Quest and Conquest

Other books by James Reeves
published by Blackie:
Exploits of Don Quixote
Fables from Aesop
Gods and Voyagers
Heroes and Monsters
Islands and Palaces
The Voyage of Odysseus

Quest and Conquest

Pilgrim's Progress retold

James Reeves

Illustrated by Joanna Troughton

BLACKIE
Glasgow and London

ISBN 0 216 90158 8

Blackie and Son Limited

Bishopbriggs, Glasgow G64 2NZ
450/452 Edgware Road, London W2 1EG

Printed in Great Britain by
Thomson Litho Limited,
East Kilbride, Scotland

Contents

Preface 9
1 The Quest Begins 11
2 Christian at the Gate 17
3 The House of Interpreter 25
4 The Hill of Difficulty 33
5 The Sisters of Charity 41
6 The Palace Beautiful 49
7 The Battle with Apollyon 55
8 The Valley of the Shadow of Death 61
9 Faithful's Story 69
10 The Talkative Pilgrim 77
11 At Vanity Fair 85
12 Christian and Faithful Imprisoned 91
13 The Trial and Death of Faithful 97
14 The Silver Snare 105
15 Doubting Castle 113
16 Giant Despair 121
17 The Delectable Mountains 129
18 The Web of Flattery 137
19 Crossing the Enchanted Ground 143
20 The Shining Ones 149
21 The Pilgrim's Conquest 155

Quest and Conquest

Preface

John Bunyan was born in 1628, the son of a Bedfordshire tinker. He learned to read and write at the village school, and as a boy he was apprenticed to his father's trade. When he was sixteen, he became a soldier, remaining for two years in the Parliamentary army which was eventually victorious in the great political and religious Civil War.

In later life John Bunyan used to say that his childhood had been idle and wicked. A change had come over him when he returned from the wars and got married. He and his wife were very poor, but she owned two religious books which they read together and which quickened John's faith. She died seven years later and he was left to bring up four young children. He laboured all day to feed them. In the evenings he preached in the open air to crowds of simple people, encouraging them to read the Bible and turn away from idleness and vanity.

This open-air preaching brought him into trouble with the authorities, and he spent many years in jail. Fortunately he had married again, and his second wife looked after the children and strove constantly to have him set free.

It was during a six-month spell in prison that Bunyan wrote the first part of *The Pilgrim's Progress*. This is his most famous work and has always been very popular. During the eighteenth and nineteenth centuries many simple homes would contain only two books—the Bible and Bunyan's masterpiece.

The Pilgrim's Progress was not written for children. Much of its dry religious discussion has little interest for modern readers. But the story of the Pilgrim, Christian, beset by danger and evil, fighting his way to safety and salvation, remains as exciting as ever. Christian's virtues of courage, resolution and goodness are qualities we can still admire.

In this version of the story, the language has been made simpler and more modern, and the dull passages of abstract debate have been left out. Christian's heroic adventures, however, the battle with Apollyon, the imprisonment in Vanity Fair, the meeting with Giant Despair, and the many other trials and tribulations of the journey, are told as Bunyan told them. It would be vain to try to improve on a story which has been read with such profound affection by people in many lands for three hundred years. The secret of its appeal lies in Bunyan's passion, sincerity and originality, and in his love of that greatest of all English classics, the King James Bible.

JR
Lewes 1975

I

The Quest Begins

As Christian lay asleep in a cave, he had a dream. The dream was of a man in rags. It was himself, Christian, and he was standing with his back to his house, reading a book. The man's shoulders were bowed, as if he carried a great burden. As he read in his book, the tears fell from his eyes and he trembled. Unable any longer to control himself, he gave a great cry.

"What shall I do?" he groaned. "Oh, what shall I do? I learn here that our city will be struck by fire from heaven, and my house will be burned to the ground. My own dear wife and children will be destroyed in that fire."

Once again Christian saw himself in the dream, walking in the fields with his eyes on the book. Again a great cry broke from him.

"What shall I do to be saved?"

He looked as if he would run from the place; yet he stood still, for he did not know which way to go. Next, Christian saw that a man named Evangelist came up to him and said,

"Why are you crying?"

"Sir," replied Christian, "I learn from this book that I am condemned to die, and afterwards to be judged. I don't want to die, and I can't face the judgement."

"But why don't you want to die," asked Evangelist,

"when this life is so full of care and sorrow?"

"Because", answered Christian, "I am afraid that this great burden at my back will drag me down lower than the grave, and I shall fall into the blackest pit of destruction. If I am unable to face such a fate, then how can I face judgement and perhaps execution? It is these thoughts which make me cry."

"Then why do you stand here?" Evangelist asked.

"Because I don't know which way to turn."

At this, Evangelist handed him a paper on which were written the words: FLY FROM THE WRATH TO COME!

When Christian had read it, he said to Evangelist,

"But where shall I fly?"

Evangelist pointed across the plain and said,

"Do you see that small gate?"

Christian shaded his eyes, looked where Evangelist pointed, and said,

"No."

"Then do you see that shining light?"

"I think I do."

Evangelist said,

"Good. Keep that light in front of you and go towards it. Then you will see the gate. Knock at the gate, and you will be told what to do."

At once Christian began to run. He had not gone far from his own door when his wife and children saw him and called out to him to come back. He put his fingers in his ears so as not to hear them, and ran on.

"Life!" he cried. "Eternal life!"

As he ran on across the plain, the neighbours also came out of their houses to see him. Some of them made fun of him, and others threatened him with raised fists. Others shouted to him to come back. Among these there were two who were determined to bring him back

by force. One was called Obstinate, for his nature was harsh and stubborn. The other was called Pliable, because he was easily persuaded to do what anyone told him. They ran after Christian and stopped him.

"Neighbours," said he, "why have you followed me?"

"To make you come back with us," they answered.

"I shan't return with you, neighbours. You live in the City of Destruction, the city of my birth. Sooner or later you will die there and fall into the burning pit. You had better come along with me."

"What?" cried Obstinate. "You want us to leave home and lose all our friends and our comforts?"

"Yes," replied Christian. "Everything you will lose is not worth the smallest part of what I am going to enjoy. If you come with me, we can all share in my happiness, for there is more than enough for all of us."

"And what is it that you want to exchange for what you're leaving behind?"

"I am going to find my birthright," Christian answered, "the happiness which awaits me in heaven. You can read about it in this book."

"Rubbish," said Obstinate. "You can keep your book. Are you coming back home with us or not?"

"No. What I've begun I will finish."

"Come on then, Neighbour Pliable," said Obstinate. "Let's go home without him. There are a lot of these pigheaded fools about, and there's no arguing with them."

"Well," said Pliable, "don't make fun of him. If what he says is true, he has more to look forward to than we have. I have a good mind to go with him."

"What?" cried Obstinate. "Are *you* one of these fools? Be sensible and come home with me. Where do you think this madman will lead you? Come home, I say."

But Pliable answered,

"Don't speak ill of our neighbour. If what he says is true, he has better things to look forward to than we have. I think I'll go along with him."

"Come home with me," Obstinate went on. "This fellow is out of his mind and may lead you into all sorts of trouble."

"We shall inherit an everlasting kingdom, he tells us," said Pliable. "There we shall enjoy everlasting life. We shall have crowns of glory, and clothes that will make us shine like the sun in heaven. There shall be no more tears, no more grief. The king of that place will wipe away all tears. But how shall we enjoy these things?"

"It is here in this book," answered Christian. "The king of that everlasting kingdom will give us all these things freely if we truly desire them."

"I'm very glad to hear this," said Pliable. "Let us hurry on our way."

"I can go no faster," said Christian, "because of the burden on my back."

Soon after this, Pliable and Christian reached the edge of a muddy slough in the middle of the plain. Obstinate had already left them and turned back in disgust. This was a great bog called the Slough of Despond. Beneath the reeds and bushes that grew in it, all was mire and slush. The two neighbours did not draw back in time, and soon found themselves wallowing in the mud. Deeper and deeper they waded until their clothes were all daubed with slime. Christian, because of the weight on his shoulders, sank until the mire reached to his waist.

"Where are you now, Neighbour Christian?" Pliable asked.

"Truly," answered Christian, "I don't know."

"Ah," said Pliable indignantly, "is this the happiness you promised? If this is how our journey begins, what can we expect before the end? All I want to do is to get out of this alive. You can have your everlasting kingdom to yourself, for all I care."

With these words he struggled hard, grasping at the reeds that grew near the edge of the slough. He dragged himself out of the mud on the edge nearest his home and off he went. And that was the last that Christian saw of him.

2

Christian at the Gate

After Pliable had disappeared from view, Christian began to struggle more and more violently to escape from the Slough. He also tried to haul himself out by grasping at the reeds, but the soft mud clung to his body and he was weighed down by the burden on his back. As he lay there panting, wondering whether he would ever stand on firm ground again, he saw a stranger making his way across the fields to the edge of the marsh.

"Good-day," said the stranger. "How do you come to be stuck in this quagmire?"

"I was longing to escape from the city," explained Christian, "and a good man called Evangelist pointed out the way to that wicket gate which you see beyond the field over there. But I seem to have gone astray right at the start of my journey. My friend Pliable, who was with me, has returned home, and I am left struggling here alone."

"My name is Help," said the stranger, stretching his arm out to Christian. "Let me pull you clear of this treacherous swamp."

Christian seized the strong arm which Help had offered him, and in no time he was standing safely on the springy turf of the field. Wishing him success in his journey, Help went back in the direction he had come from, and Christian continued towards the little gate.

But before five minutes had passed, he saw another stranger approaching him. This man had a contented and prosperous air, as if he had never felt a moment's pain or hunger. Coming up to Christian, he swept off his hat, bowed and began to speak.

"I am Mr Worldly Wiseman," he announced. "From the mud on your clothes, I would say that you have met with some misfortune on your journey. I'm always sorry to see a chap who's met with bad luck. Tell me the whole story, and we'll see if we can't help you in some way."

Christian explained that Evangelist had sent him on the path to the little gate. "I hope to be there soon," he said, "and then perhaps my troubles will be over."

"Pooh!" said Worldly Wiseman. "If you ask me, you're meddling in affairs that you know nothing about. Your troubles, as you call them, have hardly begun, my friend. I can tell you what lies in wait for you on the road. Pain and exhaustion, bitter weather and savage beasts. Your belly will be pinched with hunger and your mind half-crazed with fear long before you come to the end. I suppose you think you know what you're doing, but I don't mind admitting that I can't see the point of this famous journey of yours."

Christian pointed over his shoulder to the burden which hung heavily on his back. "To free myself from this," he said simply, "I am ready to endure any hardship."

"Fine words, fine words," said Wiseman, smiling, "but you talk like a book. If you ask me, you've been staring at the print of some old Bible until you've forgotten how to see what's in front of your nose. I expect words are the only things you can take in. Look up there," he continued, grabbing hold of Christian's arm. "I bet you can't even see what's on top of that hill."

Christian followed Wiseman's pointing finger until he saw, neatly set out on the upper slopes of a nearby hill, a small village. Everything seemed clean and orderly—although it was difficult to be sure from such a distance.

"That, my friend, is the little township of Morality. You can see for yourself what a nice quiet place it is. If you want to get rid of that burden of yours, I've got a friend living there who'll give you just the advice you want. He's a lawyer—called Mr Legality. Of course, if you really want to persevere in this wretched journey and spend God knows how long in perilous lands, that's up to you. But if you'll take a tip from me, I should just go up the hill and drop in and see my friend Legality. He'll soon put you right."

With these words, Worldly Wiseman put on his hat and walked briskly away over the fields. Christian stood for several minutes lost in thought. Should he take the advice of this man, who seemed so brisk and cheery and who clearly knew so much about life? After all, Evangelist was not the only person who could help.

Christian's mind was made up. With a light heart he turned aside from the path to the little gate and began to climb up the road to the village of Morality. But the slope, which had seemed so gentle, became steeper with every yard. Before long Christian was gasping for breath. Meanwhile the sky grew darker and a cold wind began to ruffle the spiky grass along the roadside. When he turned to look back at his route, Christian saw with a shock that the valley was almost hidden in rolling black clouds. As he stood in panic on the path, the first drops of rain fell heavily into the dust, and thunder growled among the peaks overhead. A storm was coming on, and Christian was alone on the mountain side.

When the tempest reached its height, the gloom of the

air was suddenly cleft by a brilliant flash of lightning. In the white glare, Christian saw a figure coming steadily towards him. Terror quickened his heart. He would have run away had he been able to find a foothold on the slippery rock. And now, in a second flash of lightning, he saw that the stranger had reached his side and was about to speak to him.

"Evangelist!" cried Christian, overjoyed to recognize his friend.

"Come with me," said Evangelist, taking his hand and leading him carefully down the steep track. As they descended, the storm grew quieter and the air became sweet and clear once more.

"How did you come to be so far from the right path?" asked Evangelist. He frowned as he spoke, but Christian could feel the kindness and concern which lay beneath his anger.

"I met Mr Worldly Wiseman," he explained. "He told me that the path you had sent me on was needlessly harsh, and that I could rid myself of my burden without running any dreadful risk. Like a fool I took him at his word, and set off to seek the help of a friend of his, a lawyer who lives in the village of Morality. But the path was not as easy as I had thought, and if you had not come to my rescue I am afraid that I would have met with some terrible fate."

"Christian," said Evangelist earnestly, "there are many others who will give you advice like Worldly Wiseman's. Every town is full of idiots who think they can escape destruction by sitting indoors in front of a warm fire. Human help is enough, so they think, and they have no time for journeying to strange lands. According to them, you only have to follow a few easy rules, and you can stuff your belly with roast meat and sleep on a soft feather mattress every day of your life."

Christian felt full of shame and could not look into Evangelist's eyes.

"But there is only one road," continued Evangelist. "Fortunately, although you have lost your way, I can put you back on the path. But I must warn you that if you turn aside again you may be lost for ever. Over there in the distance you can see the little gate. I will leave you now, and wish you a good journey."

Christian took Evangelist's hand and pressed it warmly. He went on his way determined that nothing would distract him. He spoke to nobody, and looked neither right nor left. In less than an hour he had arrived at the gate, above which were written the words: KNOCK AND IT SHALL BE OPENED UNTO YOU.

He knocked boldly on the wooden panelling, and almost at once heard footsteps hurrying up to the gate on the inside. A key turned in the lock, and he was standing face to face with a thin, serious-looking man dressed in grey.

"Who are you?" asked this man. "Where have you come from, and what are you looking for?"

"My name is Christian. I was longing to free myself from the heavy burden on my back, and Evangelist told me that I must undertake a journey which would begin at this gate. When I saw the words which are written up above, I knocked. I hope that you will let me pass through."

When he heard the name of Evangelist, the expression on the man's face grew softer. "I am Good-will," he said when Christian had told his tale. "I will help you through this gate. Together I am sure we can dodge the arrows of Satan."

"The arrows of Satan?" repeated Christian, puzzled.

Good-will drew Christian's attention to a gloomy castle which overlooked the gate. Built on the steep rocks of the valley side, the castle was so black and twisted that it looked like part of the precipice. This was why Christian had not noticed it earlier. But now, as he and Good-will stood gazing at it, he felt a shudder of fear run through him.

"All around the battlements, cunning archers wait to shoot their arrows," said Good-will. "When you make your way through this gate, they will fire. But you must not be afraid. I am waiting for you here. You need only step boldly towards me and you can come to no harm."

Christian paused a moment to calm himself. He felt courage grow strong within him.

"Now," said Good-will.

Christian stepped forward. At once the air was full of the hiss of flying arrows. Their deadly points flashed past his ears and he could hear them burying themselves with a thud in the woodwork of the gate. But Christian looked neither right nor left and in a few seconds he was safe inside. He looked at Good-will and could not help grinning with relief.

"You were in no danger," said Good-will.

Christian was not so sure about this, but he said nothing and listened patiently to the instructions which Good-will gave him.

"Your way is easy to recognize. There are many winding paths, but only one that runs always straight. There are many wide paths, but only one that is always narrow. Follow the straight and narrow way throughout your journey and you will arrive safely at the end. Is that clear?"

"Yes," said Christian. Good-will had walked a few yards with him, and he now saw the road which he must travel stretching away before him. How could he ever get lost, when the directions were so clear?

"Now I shall wish you success in your journey, and say farewell," said Good-will. "Before you have travelled very far, you will arrive at the house of Interpreter. When you get there, you must knock at his door, and tell him who you are."

3

The House of Interpreter

Christian walked along the straight and narrow path which Good-will had shown him until he came to the house of Interpreter. He walked up to the door and knocked boldly. A servant showed him into the hall, asked him to wait, and went off into the great dim house to fetch his master.

Christian's eyes had grown used to the sunshine, and at first he could see nothing in this hall. He heard the footsteps of the servant echoing away down a corridor. A few moments later a door opened and closed and there was the sound of voices. Then a flickering light appeared in the distance throwing dancing shadows on the walls. The light grew stronger as it grew nearer. Christian realized that it came from a candle. Now the bearer of the candle, a lean man with the lined face of a scholar, stood before him.

"Good-will told me to visit you," said Christian. "I am flying from Destruction. I want to travel to the City of Eternal Life. Can you offer me help for my journey?"

"Come with me," said Interpreter. He led the way back down the corridor, at the end of which was a circular chamber with seven doors leading out of it.

"Do you understand the meaning of my name?" asked Interpreter. "To interpret means to explain. Behind these seven doors are seven mysterious visions. We will look at them together. If they puzzle you, I will help you to make sense of them. When you have understood what you have seen, then it will be time for you to continue on your way."

With these words, Interpreter opened the first door and led Christian into the first of the seven rooms. On the opposite wall hung a picture glowing with a strong light. In the centre of the picture stood a man wearing a dazzling crown of gold. He held an open book in his hands and his eyes were gazing up at the sky. The background showed a landscape full of life: merchants haggled in a crowded market-place, labourers sweated in the fields, and idlers ate and drank outside taverns. But the man crowned with gold paid no attention to any of this, his eyes being turned constantly to Heaven.

"What is the meaning of this?" asked Christian.

"This man", said Interpreter, "is the guide who can lead you to the Eternal City. With the help of that book, he can explain the riddles which torment us. As you see, he does not fix his attention on the business of this world. He is sure of the glory which will be his in the world to come. And you, too, Christian, must learn to bear the troubles of the present for the sake of the certain rewards of the future."

They now entered the second room. As soon as the door was closed, Christian began to sneeze. There was dust all over the floor, lying thick and heavy.

"I will ask someone to sweep this room out," said Interpreter.

A man with a broom came hurrying in and began to sweep the floor with brisk strokes. The dust rose in clouds. Before, it had been getting up Christian's nose; now it made his eyes water, too, and clogged his throat until he could hardly breathe.

"Stop, stop!" cried Interpreter to the man. Then he turned to a young girl who stood nearby and asked her to fetch water. She brought a blue jug and scattered the crystal-clear drops over the floor. The dust stopped flying up to choke them. Now that it was damp, it settled on the ground and could be swept up with ease.

"Do you know the meaning of this?" asked Interpreter. Christian shook his head.

"This room is like the heart of a wicked man, thick with evil thoughts. The broom is like the Law, with its threats and punishments. As you saw, it did no good. On the contrary, Law, by filling men with anger, stirs up thoughts of hate in their hearts. But the Gospel, which speaks of Love, is like the pure water, bringing calm and order and putting an end to sin."

"Now I understand," said Christian. "Shall we go to the third room?"

In this third room sat two boys. They looked so alike that Christian decided they must be brothers. But in their behaviour they were quite different from one another. The elder of the two—whose name, said Interpreter, was Passion—writhed and wriggled in his chair as if it were an ants' nest. His face twitched with restlessness and he cast his eyes wildly about the room. Meanwhile Patience, his younger brother, sat quietly, seeming perfectly contented.

"Passion is greedy for the things of this world," said Interpreter. "His impatience torments him. When he gets his hands on something which he has been longing for, he can never enjoy it, because he has to devour it as quickly as he can. You see that a man is bringing him a sack of gold at this moment. He plunges his hands into the sack, and his mind glows with thoughts of the fine clothes he will buy and the rich meals he will eat. But as his fists close on the coins, they slip through his fingers like water. If he wants to spend this gold, he must do so in a mad rush, before it is gone for ever. So he ends up as you see him—still in ragged clothes, and frantic with rage and unsatisfied greed."

"His brother Patience has no gold at all," said Christian.

"Patience is happy to wait. He has fixed his thoughts on the world to come. He knows that those things which can be bought with gold are in truth worthless. At the moment Passion may seem a lucky man—though you can see for yourself that his riches have not brought him peace of mind. But Patience knows that a time is coming when everything will be turned upside down. The man who is first now will be last then. Those who have nothing—men like Patience—will receive their reward, for those who were last will then be first."

Christian could make no sense at all of the scene which met his eyes as he entered the fourth room. A sweet fire burned in the hearth. A demon dressed all in black, his mouth twisted with hate, flung pail after pail of water on to the flames, but they only flared up with a clearer light. The black demon cursed and swore, pouring on more water, but his task was hopeless.

Christian frowned. "I don't understand. Why does the fire burn on so strongly?"

"Look there," said Interpreter, pointing. "At the side of the hearth, standing quietly in the corner, is Christ. He feeds the flames with oil. This fire is the fire of Love, which the Devil longs to drown in hate and wickedness. But the grace of Christ, poured out like oil, keeps the fire blazing in our hearts. As long as he feeds it, it can never die."

The fifth room was full of magnificent light. Christian

thought he had never been in such a beautiful place. In the distance was a castle whose walls shone like silver. On the towers and battlements of the castle men and women walked up and down, their faces bright with joy.

"We will go closer," said Interpreter. "Watch carefully, and try to understand what you see."

Christian saw that a great crowd of people streamed towards the gates of the shining palace. They all longed to enter. But on the narrow drawbridge leading up to the doorway stood a band of armed men. They held swords of sharp steel, and whenever anyone drew near they rushed out with hideous screams and yells. Terrified, the travellers abandoned their hopes and fled from the castle.

Then one man, bolder and more determined than the rest, stepped forward onto the drawbridge. The armed men fell on him, but he was a match for them all. His courage did not fail him. He drew his own shining weapon and fought his way to the door. As soon as he stood before it, it was opened from within. The brave man was welcomed into the palace with triumphant music and heavenly singing.

"This time I think I do understand," said Christian. "On the road to the heavenly palace, sin and peril, wicked thoughts, and dangerous passions, lurk like highwaymen, ready to attack and destroy the timid traveller. But whoever is bold enough to fight off these enemies will arrive safely at his goal."

Interpreter smiled. "You are learning, my friend," he said.

"And now," said Christian, "let me continue on my way. Everything that I have seen has strengthened my eagerness to be on the road again. I can wait no longer."

"There are two more visions that you must see," said Interpreter gravely. "Then you will be ready to set out."

The sixth vision turned Christian's blood cold with horror. In the middle of a dank, murky room stood a cage, its bars made of solid iron. You would have expected to find some fierce beast locked up inside it. But the sound which Christian heard was not the growling of a lion or tiger. It was the sighing of a man.

"I am a man of despair," said the prisoner. "Once I was full of hope. Like you, I set out for the Eternal City. But look at me now. I began to live a life of wickedness. I turned away from the light and strayed off the true path. Now I am in this cage for ever. I cannot get out. No, I cannot escape."

As he spoke, he shook the iron bars until they rattled. But his hands were feeble, and the bars were massive. It was clearly true: as he said, he was doomed to remain for ever in his prison.

"God help me to keep clear of the sins which have brought that man to such an end," murmured Christian as they left the room. "And now, I beg you to let me go on my way."

"There is still one more sight for you to see," said Interpreter. "When I open the seventh door, you will see a man waking from sleep. He has just been dreaming of the Day of Judgement. He has lived such a wicked life that he knew in his dream that he had no hope of entering the City of Salvation. Instead, Hell yawned before him with all its horrors."

In the seventh room, Christian saw a bed against the wall. As they opened the door, a man sprang from the sheets with a cry of fright. He stared desperately into the empty air, and his legs trembled so violently that he could barely stand up. He wrung his hands in despair and sweat poured from his forehead.

"Even in a dream," said Interpreter, "he has been so

terrified by the thought of Judgement that he has almost lost his wits. He was not ready: his sins still lay heavily on his shoulders. Let us hope that you, Christian, will be ready."

They went back into the circular chamber and Interpreter, holding his candle up to light the way, led Christian down the long corridor. The door was opened and Christian stood on the step. When he saw the open country, the wide sky and the straight, narrow path leading onwards, his heart was filled with joy and longing.

"Now I will go on my way," he said to Interpreter. "But do not think that I will forget the lessons that I have learned here. I will always think gratefully of your kindness to me."

"If you are tempted to leave the true path," said Interpreter, "think of what you have been shown. Let the visions you have seen put hope and fear in your heart."

Interpreter then wished Christian success and said farewell. With firm steps, Christian continued on his journey.

4

The Hill of Difficulty

When he had left Interpreter's house, Christian, who was in a great hurry to continue his journey, began to run along the path. He found himself climbing a steep track on either side of which rose high walls. Run as he might, he still felt that his progress was too slow, for he was weighed down by the burden of sin upon his back.

Gasping for breath, he paused to wipe the sweat from his forehead.

"How I wish I were free of this heavy burden!" he sighed. "Then my journey would be twice as quick."

As he spoke, he looked about, and saw a green hill rising up before him. On the top of this hill stood a wooden cross. Christian's eyes began to overflow with tears, until everything he saw was swimming in a mist. He felt his body fill with a calm joy. As he gazed at the shining cross, the burden which had clung to him for so many miles was lifted from him as if by an invisible hand. Christian watched it roll bouncing down the slope of the hill. When it reached the bottom, it disappeared into the mouth of a cave, which was half hidden by a huge boulder.

"Thanks to this cross and this cave," said Christian, "my burden has been taken from me. How much more easily I will travel now."

Three figures dressed in dazzling robes came up to him

where he stood. The first spoke kindly, telling him that he was forgiven for all the wrong that he had ever done. The second took the rags from his back. In place of his tattered clothes, he was given a fine clean coat. The third shining figure handed him a roll of parchment covered with beautiful writing and sealed with wax.

"Take this scroll," he said. "Read it during your journey. When you arrive at the gate of the Eternal City, hand it to the porter."

The third figure also touched Christian's forehead, leaving a mark there which could never be washed off. Then the three beings disappeared and he was left to continue on his way.

Before he had gone very far, he came across three men who lay snoring in a ditch, their legs bound with iron chains.

"Wake up!" cried Christian. "This place may be full of dangerous beasts. Some lion, prowling for food, may devour you as you lie here."

The three men rubbed their eyes and yawned.

"I can't see any danger," said the first, whose name was Simple.

The second man said, "It's not for nothing that people call me Sloth. You may be right in what you say. But I'm going to sleep a bit longer before I budge."

The third man was a big-headed fellow. "Follow your own advice," he said, "and I'll do the same. Folks call me Presumption, because I never listen to what others tell me. Well, I'm not going to change at my time of life."

Christian went sadly on his way. The three men had not even thanked him for his warning. He realized that the road was crowded with wayfarers, some foolish, some wicked, some proud or idle,

He was roused from his thoughts by a sudden shouting and clattering on his left. Looking round to see what was happening, he saw two men sliding and tumbling down the steep wall. They fell in a heap at his feet, but soon scrambled up and brushed the dust off their clothes.

"Where have you come from?" asked Christian. "Where are you going to?"

"My name is Formalist," said the taller of the two. "My friend is called Hypocrisy. We got fed up with our own country, so we thought we'd pay a visit to the City of Zion. I expect they'll be glad to see us."

"Oh, yes," said Hypocrisy. "They'll put on a big banquet in our honour, I should think."

"I, too, am going to that City," said Christian. "Unlike you, I came in through the gate. I'm surprised that you dared scramble over the wall like that. The Lord of the City will certainly be very angry with you."

Hypocrisy smiled. "Rubbish. People have got in over the wall for years. Everybody does it."

"Besides," said Formalist, "the main thing is to get in. I don't see what odds it makes whether we came through the front door, the back door or any other door."

"Very well," said Christian. "You can make up your own rules as you go. I shall follow the rules laid down by the Lord."

The three of them walked some way in silence. To tell the truth, Christian did not particularly want to talk to these travellers.

"Look here," said Hypocrisy suddenly. "There's only one thing you've got that we haven't—your coat. It's a nice new coat, I'll admit. I suppose the neighbours gave it to you when your old one fell to bits, because they didn't want to watch you walking about naked."

Formalist and Hypocrisy began to laugh loudly, but

Christian, instead of losing his temper, gave them a serious reply.

"You're right about one thing. My old rags certainly were falling to pieces. But my new coat was given to me by the Lord of this place. I wear it to remind myself of his goodness. When I arrive at the Heavenly City, I shall be recognized by this coat. I was given other signs, too: this mark here on my forehead, and this roll of parchment which I carry with me to read on the way."

They had arrived at the foot of another hill. It did not seem possible that a man could climb such a steep and rocky slope. The straight path led sheer up the face of the mount. To the left and right ran other tracks, broad and easy.

"Well, friends, this is the path for me," said Hypocrisy, striding away down the left-hand track. He did not know it, but his way led him into a perilous wood from which he was not to escape with his life.

"I'll try the other one, I think," said Formalist. "Good-bye, then."

Waving and smiling, he set off down the right-hand path. He did not know it, but he was headed for the Mountains of Destruction where he would fall to his death among icy black rocks.

Christian went on his way alone. Even without his burden, it was stiff work climbing the mountain path. After a few minutes, he found it impossible to walk upright. He was forced to go down on his hands and knees, gripping the rocks with his fingers and pulling himself along slowly and painfully.

"I know that this is the only way," he thought, "but I would dearly like to lie down for a while and get back my strength."

Just as he was thinking this, the path levelled out, and

he found himself on the edge of a meadow of thick grass full of brightly-coloured flowers. In the shade of a leafy tree stood a wooden bench. Christian heard the delightful sound of running water. From the rocks behind the tree flowed a clear spring, which trickled down over the stones before falling into a shining pool.

Christian gave thanks for his good fortune, drank deeply from the pool among the rocks, and stretched himself out on the bench. He took out his scroll and began to read from the beautiful text. But the words seemed to float before his eyes. His thoughts began to wander. His eyes closed and he lay on the bench in the shade, snoring.

His sleep did not last long, however. A mighty voice boomed suddenly in his ears.

"You lazy good-for-nothing! Even the humble ant makes good use of her time. But you lie here as if you had been guzzling rich food at a feast and waste your time in sleep."

Christian leapt to his feet and stared around the meadow. There was no one to be seen. The voice which had woken him must have been sent in a dream. He had been warned against laziness; he must make haste to be on his way. Without a backward glance he set off once more up the harsh rocks of the mountain side.

All at once he was knocked off his feet by two strangers who came tearing down the path towards him. All three lay sprawling on the rocks. Christian noticed that the strangers were white with terror.

"What has frightened you?" he asked. "What makes you come rushing down the mountain side like madmen, knocking honest travellers down?"

The two men could scarcely speak for fright and breathlessness.

"M–m–my name is M–M–Mistrust," stammered the

first one. He pointed to his friend. "This is T–T–Timorous. We were walking——" And he began to sob and blubber so that Christian could no longer understand a word that he said.

"L–l–lions," said Timorous. "We saw two lions. They were in the road, right in front of us. Oh!" And he too began to moan and shiver.

"Lions are not the best of company for travellers," agreed Christian. "I can see the danger of pressing on up this hill. But if I go back, I know for sure that destruction waits for me. At least I can hope for safety if I continue on my way."

"But the f–f–further you go," said Timorous, "the w–w–worse it gets."

And the two cowards rushed off down the path as fast as they could. They slithered on the rocks and bruised and cut themselves on the sharp stones, but their panic was stronger than any fear of hurting themselves.

As for Christian, he went boldly on. He did not want to meet with wild beasts, but he knew that to turn back was the most certain death of all.

"I will look at my scroll," he thought, "to cheer myself up."

He reached into his breast pocket for the precious roll of parchment. It was gone! He had lost it, and now how would he gain entrance to the Eternal City? His whole journey was wasted!

Overcome with despair, Christian sat down at the side of the road and wept bitterly.

"I will lie here till nightfall," he said, "and then I will freeze to death. At least that will be an end to my troubles."

This mood passed in time, and he began to think carefully back over all that had happened to him since he had been given the scroll. Suddenly he realized what he had done: in his haste to leave the meadow, after his shameful sleep, he had left the scroll behind!

He turned and ran down the path. Until he had the parchment in his hands again, he could not rest. He regretted his folly and forgetfulness, and the time he was forced to waste in retracing his own steps—but there was no choice. The scroll was his pass into the City, and he must find it or perish.

Entering the meadow once more, he rushed over to the bench under the tree. At first he saw no sign of what he was looking for and his heart grew sick with worry. Then, gleaming white in the long grass, he saw it. Seizing it in his trembling hands, Christian gave thanks that he had found the priceless scroll and could go on his way.

How much easier the climb now seemed. Christian felt like singing with joy. The sunset flooded the sky with golden streams as he stepped lightly up the hill.

"It is almost dark," he thought, "and lions are prowling. But perhaps I shall find some safe place to spend the night."

He looked round in the dusk. To his left rose a stately palace, its vast windows glowing with light. This noble building had risen in a moment, as if by magic.

"Here perhaps I will find a welcome," thought Christian. And he began to walk up the passage which led to the castle gate.

5

The Sisters of Charity

Before he could reach the bright lights of the Palace Beautiful, Christian had to walk in darkness up the narrow passage to the gate. He listened keenly for any sound which might warn him of danger and kept a firm hold on the hilt of his sword.

Suddenly, when he had almost reached the entrance, he heard a low, snuffling noise. It was the breathing of a wild beast. As Christian stood terrified and motionless on the path, the snuffling became a snorting. Then he heard a violent roar. The beasts—for there were two of them—were lions. Timorous and Mistrust had warned him of the danger. It had been easy enough to talk bravely on the hill side in daylight, but now his heart was thudding with fright and he too longed to run away.

"What shall I do?" he cried. He took one cautious step and the roaring became more savage than ever. "Death is right in front of me. I have no choice but to fly!"

As he turned to run, a deep voice rang out from the darkness.

"Is your courage so slight? I am Watchful, the porter who keeps this gate, and I am waiting to let you in. Are you such a coward as to be put to flight by a pair of chained lions?"

"I didn't know they were chained," said Christian.

"But in any case, surely they will leap out and pin me to the ground. Once they have me down, their chains will hardly prevent them from eating me."

"You faint-hearted man!" said Watchful. "The lions are put beside the path as a test of faith. If you fail this test, you will get no further in your journey, my friend."

"Very well," declared Christian, drawing his sword. "I will walk on." But as he spoke, the lions growled furiously and he trembled to hear them.

"Keep to the middle of the path, and you will come to no harm," said Watchful. "I am waiting here to welcome you."

Although he could not altogether master his fear, Christian controlled the shaking of his legs and began to walk deliberately forward. The chains rattled as the maddened beasts strained to attack him. He heard the gnashing of their teeth and felt their hot breath on his face. But the lions' struggles were in vain, for Christian passed them by and stepped up unharmed to the gate of the Palace Beautiful.

"I have come from the City of Destruction," said Christian, "and I am on my way to Zion. It grew dark as I climbed the hill and I thought that in this place I might find shelter for the night."

"Why have you arrived so late?" asked Watchful. "The sun set some time ago. Travellers usually come while it is still light."

"Wretch that I am, I fell asleep on a bench while I was reading my scroll. I hurried on when I awoke, but then I found that I had left the scroll behind me. I had to go back for it. If I had been less lazy and forgetful, I would have been here long ago."

"Well," said the porter, "this palace was built by the

Lord of the Hill as a shelter for travellers. You have chosen the right gate to knock at."

He drew back the bolt and let Christian in. The two lions, who had been moaning and growling in their hungry rage, gave a last howl of disappointment and fell silent.

Watchful pulled a rope which hung against the wall. Far off in the inner rooms of the palace a bell jangled.

"I have summoned one of the maidens who live here," he explained. "When she has seen you, and talked to you awhile, she will decide whether or not you are to be made welcome."

Christian heard footsteps and saw a lantern being carried down the garden path to the gate. A beautiful girl, who said her name was Discretion, came up to Christian and asked what had made him come to the Palace.

Christian told her what he had already told the porter. "I am even keener to stay here," he added, "now that I know that this palace was built by the Lord as a shelter for people like myself, travellers overtaken by the night."

The girl smiled kindly at Christian. "Indeed," she said, "you are just the kind of guest we most warmly welcome. Come into our house, and I will call my three sisters. They are called Prudence, Piety, and Charity, and I know that they are always eager to hear stories told by pilgrims and wayfarers."

She led him into a brightly lit room in the palace. A fire burned cheerfully in the grate, and the air was perfumed with sweet smoke. Christian, who was footsore and exhausted, sighed with pleasure as he sat down before the flames.

Discretion left the room and a few moments later came back with refreshing drinks set out in silver goblets on

a tray of carved wood, which she held out to Christian.

"I expect you are hungry," she said. "Before long, we will eat. Meanwhile rest yourself here, and drink something cool. I will leave you now, but my sisters will be coming to talk with you."

The first of the other maidens to come into the room was Piety. Her dark hair hung down her back, and she wore a plain, grey gown. Sitting down beside him, she asked Christian what had first made him set out on his journey.

"I knew that Destruction would fall on me if I remained in my own country. A good man called Evangelist pointed out the way by which I could save myself and I followed the path he had shown."

"Have you had many adventures so far?" asked Piety. "I suppose you must have visited the house of Interpreter. Do you remember the sights you saw while you were there?"

Christian said he remembered them all—especially the fire which could not be put out, the man of despair in his grim cage, and the wretch who woke in terror from his dream of Judgement.

"And what else have you seen in your travels?"

"I saw three fools who lay in a ditch, snoring and bound in chains. They would not move even though I warned them of the risks they ran. Then I saw two wicked men who climbed over the wall because they did not want to enter through the gate. But they were not with me very long. The straight and narrow path was too hard for them and they branched off along tracks of their own. Finally I met with two cowards, who ran trembling from the lions at your gate. I myself came close to taking the same wretched course, but the good porter Watchful encouraged me, and I stepped boldly in."

Prudence now came over to the fireside, moving steadily and gracefully across the polished floor.

"Tell me," she said, "do you never think of your home, the land which you have left behind you?"

"Indeed I do," replied Christian. "I think of it with shame and loathing. I am on my way to a better place. I wish to forget the past and fix my thoughts on the Eternal City."

"What?" said Prudence. "Do you mean to say that you have completely changed? Surely you still feel the same longings and desires as you have always felt?"

"Alas, you are right. Greed and selfishness torment me as they used to do. But if I could control my thoughts, I would never dwell on that time." Christian sighed deeply. "Sometimes I feel that I *am* changed," he went on. "Four things help me to keep my determination strong. I think of the cross which I saw earlier today; of the scroll and the coat given me by the shining ones; and of the road which runs before me. Then my heart is full of joy and hope."

"One more question," said Prudence. "Why are you so eager to reach the City of Zion? What do you expect to find there?"

"I long to find the man who lifted from my back the burden of sin," explained Christian. "He dwells in that City, along with all those who love him. My highest wish is to become one of that happy crowd, and to live among them in bliss for ever."

Charity, the fourth sister, now entered. She was more beautiful than either Piety or Prudence. She was dressed in a gown of blue and had free-flowing, golden hair.

"When you left your home," she asked, "did you leave a wife and children behind you?"

"I did," said Christian sadly. "I begged them to come

with me, but they would not. They said I was a fool for setting out on my dangerous journey and called out to me to come back. I had to block my ears against their cries, though it wrung my heart to leave them."

"Surely you loved them? It must have been hard to abandon them in the City of Destruction."

Christian groaned. "Don't remind me! I did all I could to convince them that I was right. My actions as well as my words showed that I was no fool but a man determined to do what was best. Still they mocked me and said that I was a simpleton who didn't know how to enjoy himself. In the end, I think my goodness must have put them off more than any wickedness could have done. They loved the life they led in the City and nothing could part them from its pleasures."

Charity smiled at Christian with tender pity. "I understand, my friend," she said. "However much one loves people, there are times when one can do nothing for them. But it must have been a painful choice."

Christian groaned again and felt the tears welling up in his eyes.

"Enough of this gloomy talk," said Charity. "You are tired and hungry. Come, we will sit down and eat. And while we eat we can tell stories of the Lord of this country, a glorious hero whose deeds are joyful to speak of."

Christian's appetite had been kindled by the smell of cooking and he was more than ready to dine. He took his place at the table and was delighted to see the fine food which was placed before him—roast meat, fresh vegetables, and brown bread spread with creamy butter. Charity poured him a glass of wine and begged him to begin his meal. He needed no further encouragement.

While he ate, the maidens of the Palace spoke of the Lord.

"He is the greatest warrior there has ever been," said one. "He fought with Death and won the victory, though he shed his own blood before he triumphed. And he did all this out of love."

Another said that he had no pride in his greatness and often chose to go about in rags. "He could dwell forever in his splendid palace of Zion. But he prefers to travel the roads, giving help to those who are in need."

"He is the firmest friend a poor pilgrim could have," said the third maiden. "He has made a pilgrim into a prince before now—a man who never owned a penny in his life. Remain faithful to him, Christian, and he will remain faithful to you."

They talked late into the night, until the candles burned low and Christian's eyes began to close. He had walked many miles since morning, and he longed for sleep.

"Come," said Charity. "It is late, and you are tired. Let me show you to your chamber."

He was given a large room whose windows faced east. The sun would wake him in the morning and his strength would be fresh.

"Before you leave this place," said Charity, "there are wonderful things for you to see. But lie now in this feather bed, and sleep in peace."

6

The Palace Beautiful

The morning sun shone through the windows of Christian's room and woke him from a deep and perfect sleep. Full of strength, he leapt out of bed. Breakfast had been prepared for him. While he ate it, Discretion, Piety, Prudence and Charity explained the marvellous sights which they would show him during the day.

"I am longing to be on my way," he said, "but you have made me so welcome that I will willingly stay here and look at these wonders with you."

Everything which they showed him had to do with the Lord. All proved him to be a mighty hero, greater even than Christian had realized.

The first room he entered contained scores of documents, yellow with age. The writing was in a strange hand, but Discretion helped him to follow its meaning.

"You see from these papers," she said, "that the Lord comes from the oldest family on earth, and that he himself has existed since the beginning of time. He lived before the world was made. Kings and Princes can trace their families back for centuries, but our Lord is older by far than human history. To him, the whole of time is no more than a single day."

Piety then led Christian into a second room. Here he read stories of the miracles which had been performed by the servants of the Lord. He had never heard such marvels—the mouths of lions silenced, fire quenched in all its blazing fury, sharp swords flashing harmlessly past the bodies of heroic warriors. The stories were illustrated with brilliantly coloured pictures and beautiful tapestries hung on the walls.

"In this third room," said Charity, opening another door, "you will see that the Lord is merciful as well as mighty. Do you remember the man of despair who sat in the iron cage at the house of Interpreter? Here is a picture of a wretch who was almost as wicked as that man."

Christian looked at the book which she held. He saw an evil-looking ruffian, his face black with scorn and anger.

"This man did all he could to offend the Lord," said Charity. "His life was famous for its villainy and sin. But in the end he was overcome with sorrow for his wickedness and begged to be forgiven. His wish was granted at once and without question. Look around and you will see that there have been many others like him."

The wall was covered with paintings of desperate rogues, each more hateful than the last.

"And do you mean to say that all these have been forgiven?" asked Christian in astonishment.

"Their stories are set down in these books," said Charity. "Read and you will see. Each one of them implored the Lord to forgive him; not one did he refuse."

The fourth room was rather different from the others. It did not contain documents and pictures, but was an armoury—a room full of swords, shields and other weapons. There were shining breast-plates and helmets, greaves of strong steel, and deadly spears. Wherever he looked, Christian's eyes were dazzled by gleaming metal.

"There is enough here for a whole army!" he said.

"Yes," said Prudence. "There are weapons here for every single servant of the Lord. Before you leave our Palace, you too will be given a suit of armour from this store."

Then she took him over to a case in the corner of the room, in which were displayed several old and curious weapons. Among them was the ass's jaw-bone with which the mighty Samson had fought.

"And this," said Prudence, "is the sling with which the boy David slew Goliath."

Christian had been so fascinated by what the sisters had shown him that he had not noticed how the time was passing. To his amazement, it was dusk when he left the armoury. The evening meal was as good as it had been the day before. Afterwards they all sat talking until the candles burned low. Christian went up to his room, lay down on the bed and fell into a deep sleep.

When he woke up in the morning, he was overjoyed to think that now he would set off once more on his journey to the Eternal City. It was a day of heavy, grey cloud, but this could not damp Christian's spirit.

"And now," he said at breakfast, "I shall bid you farewell, my kind friends, and leave this palace where I have been made so welcome."

"We will not force you to stay," said Piety. "But I know that you will not regret it if you remain for one more day. Tomorrow may dawn bright and clear, and from your bedroom window you can see a most beautiful sight—the Delectable Mountains spread before you in the distance."

"What are these mountains?"

"The pilgrim's road is not only a way of sharp rocks," said Charity. "It passes through pleasant places too. These mountains are rich in vines and in fruit of every sort.

Ancient trees grow on their slopes, moved by cool breezes.
Streams trickle through green meadows and pastures
bright with flowers."

"I would love to see this view," admitted Christian.
"Do you think I dare delay any longer?"

"I understand your impatience," said Discretion. "But
there is much still to see in the Palace. Stay one day
more. Tomorrow you will be on your way. I am sure
that the dawn will be a fine one, but even if it is not,
we shall not ask you to remain with us any longer."

"Very well," said Christian. He spent the day looking
once more at the marvels of the Palace, and went early
to bed, wanting a good night's rest before the next day's
journey.

In the morning, Charity came into his room. Together
they looked from his window at the far-off Delectable
Mountains. They seemed quite close in the clear air of
the morning. The fresh green woods, the flashing water
of lakes and streams, the terraces of vineyards and
orchards—Christian saw them all with joy and wonder.

"Before you reach the Eternal City," said Charity,
"you will travel through that fruitful country."

"Yes," said Christian, "and now I will set out, for
although my stay here has been delightful, it has been
long enough."

The maidens would not let Christian leave the Palace
by himself. They knew that he must now descend into
the dreadful Valley of Humiliation, and wanted to come
part of the way with him, to give him courage.

"Have any pilgrims passed the door this morning?"
he asked Watchful as they went out through the gate.

"One man went by," said the porter. "I asked his
name, and he replied that he was called Faithful."

"Faithful!" cried Christian. "I know him well. He is a

neighbour of mine, and has long been a friend. When did he pass?"

"By now he will have reached the foot of the hill. Perhaps, if all goes well, you will meet with one another later in your journey."

Christian and Watchful said good-bye, and the pilgrim went on his way. Difficult as it had been to climb the hill, it was worse going down on the other side. Christian was glad that the maidens were at his side.

"It is a hard way down into the Valley of Humiliation," said Prudence, "and you are almost certain to slip and fall."

He did slip two or three times, but climbed to his feet again and struggled on. When they reached the bottom of the hill, the maidens of the Palace gave their guest gifts for the journey. There was a loaf of bread, some wine in a leather bottle, and a bunch of dried grapes.

"Good-bye, my friends," said Christian, taking each of them by the hand. "I will never forget you, or the kindness you showed me while I was with with you."

"Good-bye, Christian. Whatever dangers you meet, be of good courage. We know that you will bring your journey to a successful end."

With these words Discretion, Piety, Prudence and Charity left him and began to climb the hill back to the Palace Beautiful.

Christian was overcome with loneliness and fear as he took his first steps in the dark valley. He felt that some dreadful struggle lay before him.

"At least I am protected by my new armour," he thought. For he had been given a shining suit just as Prudence had promised. It was armour of an unusual kind. His front was covered by it from head to foot, but at the back he was as defenceless as if he had been naked.

"If I do meet with some monster, I shall have no choice but to stand and fight," he thought. "If I once turn tail, I am done for."

For a short while he walked on without meeting a single living creature. With every step he took he felt more strongly that a terrible enemy lay in wait. He looked anxiously on all sides, and his ears were strained with listening for any sound of danger.

Suddenly, far across the dreary fields, he saw a sight which turned his blood to ice. A great pair of wings, black as night, flapped heavily in the still air. The monster from whose back they sprouted was making his way steadily in Christian's direction, breathing thunderously as he came. His body was coated in slimy scales and fire and smoke poured forth from his belly. His feet were like a bear's, covered with rough hair and armed with vicious claws.

"I cannot run from him," said Christian. "He would fling a dart of fire at me, and my armour will not protect me if I turn my back. I must wait until he is nearer and speak with him. If it comes to a battle, I shall have to trust in the Lord's help."

The grim creature grew larger as he approached. The stench of burning flooded Christian's nostrils. This was Apollyon, the fiend with the cruel mouth of a lion. He dwelt in the Valley of Humiliation and he had slain thousands of unfortunate pilgrims. Christian could only wait, praying that he would not be the creature's next victim.

7

The Battle with Apollyon

Apollyon flew on across the field until Christian stood in the shadow of his wings. Looking through the smoke which swirled around him, the pilgrim saw that the face of his enemy was black with scorn. He tightened his grip on the hilt of his new sword. But the time to fight had not yet come; before attacking him with fiery darts, the fiend tempted Christian with wicked words.

"Where do you come from?" he asked. "Where are you going?"

"I come from the City of Destruction and I am bound for Zion."

"Destruction!" roared Apollyon. "I am the Prince of that country. All who live there are subject to my commands. How dare you run away from your birthplace! If I didn't know that you will soon be going back, I would strike you dead to punish you for your treachery."

"It is true that I was born in your Kingdom," said Christian. "I have had a taste of your service and the wages that you pay. As soon as I was able to think for myself, I made up my mind to seek a better master."

The fiend's eyes glared angrily. "You are a fool. Why should your new master be any better than your old? Come back to me and I will give you the best gifts that my Kingdom can provide."

"My new master is the King of Kings. I have promised

myself to him and I would be a traitor indeed if I went back on my word. And what is more, Apollyon, you foul fiend, I have come to love the Lord's service. I love my fellow servants, and my new country. The Lord pays me the wages of life, but when I worked for you my reward was death."

Christian spoke fearlessly and kept his eyes fixed on the monster's hideous visage. His frankness and courage were beginning to enrage his adversary.

"Very well, press on! But if you serve the Lord, remember that I am your deadly enemy. Most of his servants come to a bad end, for I use all my power to destroy them. What is more, he never lifts a finger to help them. If one of *my* followers is in trouble, on the other hand, I'm always ready to come to the rescue—I'll willingly bribe judges or poison troublesome witnesses to keep my friends out of jail."

Christian answered in a voice full of contempt. "The servants of the Lord do not care about the fate they meet in this wicked world. They are content to wait for certain glory in the world to come. If the Lord offers no help when we are in difficulty, this is to test our love, and to discover who will be faithful to the end. Whoever shows constant faith will be rewarded in Heaven."

"Very fine talk," sneered Apollyon. "However, since you set out on your journey, you have already failed three or four times in your duty to your new master. You snored through a whole afternoon and then left behind your precious scroll. A couple of mangy lions almost sent you scurrying off home like the coward you are. And if you have managed to get this far, it's not out of love for the Lord, but because you're such a braggart. You simply want to collect a nice string of adventures to boast of in your old age."

"All that you say is true," replied the pilgrim. "Anyone who sets out from Destruction is certain to be full of wickedness and vanity. Indeed, I am guilty of more faults than you have mentioned. But the Lord is merciful and he has pardoned me for all the wrong I have done."

At this Apollyon gave a horrible roar. "How I hate the Lord and all his laws, and all his servants! Christian, I am his most determined enemy, and I have come out this morning full of hate. I have come out to fight with you and destroy you."

Christian answered boldly, "Apollyon, beware what you do, for I am in the King's Highway, the Way of Holiness. Look to your own defence."

Apollyon spread his huge body across the narrow path. Christian's way was blocked by the glittering scales of the fiend's belly and his eyes were smarting with reeking smoke. The moment for battle had come.

"Prepare to die," snarled Apollyon. "By my home in Hell I swear that you will go no further."

With these words he flung a dart of fire at Christian. It came hissing through the air towards the pilgrim's heart, but he parried it with his shining shield. A great cloud of black smoke rolled from the fiend's belly, and he gave another roar. Raising himself on his black wings, he began to pour down on Christian a ceaseless hail of darts.

For hours the battle raged. The sun rose in the sky and began to sink again as afternoon drew on towards evening. There was no end to Apollyon's fury nor to the flaming missiles which he hurled. Christian stood his ground valiantly, protecting himself with his shield and never once turning his back. Neither the man nor the fiend seemed able to gain the advantage.

Heroically as Christian fought, however, he could not

defend himself from every dart. He was wounded first in the head and blood trickled down over his forehead in a scarlet stream. Then his side was pierced by a second missile. A third scored a deep cut in one of his feet, so that it was agony for him to move.

Lamed by this third wound and weak from loss of blood, Christian was forced to yield ground. Closer and closer the fiend pressed, and more and more desperate grew Christian's defence. Finally, when the fight had been going on for more than six hours, Apollyon saw his chance.

Gathering his strength, he flung himself upon the pilgrim and threw him to the ground. As he fell, Christian lost his grip on his sword. He lay pinned to the earth, the fiend above him pressing down with all his weight. Christian, struggling for breath, thought that his last hour had come.

"Now I have you!" cried Apollyon. "You will not escape me now!"

But the Lord gave Christian a last burst of strength. As the monster was lifting his sharp claws for the fatal blow, Christian reached for his sword, scrabbling with his fingertips on the hard ground. When the weapon was in his grasp once more, he gave a shout of triumph.

"Do not exult too soon, my enemy! I may have fallen, but I shall rise again."

And he thrust the shining blade deep into the fiend's flesh. Apollyon fell back as if he had received his death-blow. Christian followed up with another thrust and another, crying out that through the strength of the Lord he was greater than any warrior.

As the sharp blade struck home for the third time, Apollyon gave a groan of anguish and despair. He knew that he was beaten. His only hope was to flee before

Christian made an end of him. Struggling to his feet, he spread his huge wings and flew across the fields, retreating in shame and defeat.

At last Christian could breathe quietly. His face had been strained with the fury of the combat, but now he smiled in triumph, and looked gratefully up at the sky.

"I will give thanks to the Lord", he said, "who has helped me to walk boldly past savage lions and who has delivered me from the hands of the fiend Apollyon."

Although he had won such a great victory, he was feeble from loss of blood.

"If only some kind nurse would come and bandage these wounds!" he groaned.

As he spoke, he saw a marvellous sight. In the air beside him appeared a hand. It was the hand of an angel, glowing with light; in its fingers were clasped cool, green leaves from the Tree of Life. The battle-weary pilgrim took bunches of the leaves and held them to his wounds. At once the flow of blood was stemmed and he felt full of health and vigour.

"Now I shall eat and drink," he said, "and go on my way."

He sat down sipping the wine and munching the bread which his friends had given him that morning. He knew that he must refresh himself for he might meet with more enemies before he left the Valley of Humiliation.

"And even if I do not," he said, "I must keep my courage high, for my road runs now through another grim country. Soon I must enter the Valley of the Shadow of Death, a desert place among whose rocks no human being can live for long. Only pilgrims like myself, servants of the Lord, dare to pass through, so desolate and perilous is the way."

8

The Valley of the Shadow of Death

Grasping his sword, Christian walked on through the Valley of Humiliation until he had reached the narrow entrance to the Valley of the Shadow of Death. He knew that his strength would be as sorely tried here as it had been in the battle with Apollyon, and he stood awhile in the road summoning up his courage.

Two men came running towards him, their faces white with fear. As they ran they threw terrified glances over their shoulders. It was clear that they were flying from some dreadful danger.

"Where are you going?" asked Christian.

"Back! Back!" they cried. "If you care for your own life, come with us."

"Why, what's the matter?"

"We were going the same way as you—indeed, we went as far as we dared," said the first man.

"If we had gone any further," said the other, "we would never have returned to tell you about it."

"What have you met with?" asked Christian.

"We had almost arrived in the Valley of the Shadow of Death, which lies before you now. By good fortune we looked ahead and saw the danger in time."

"And what did you see?" asked Christian.

"Goblins and hobgoblins, goat-men and dragons," said one.

"The place is full of howling and screaming," said the other. "The sky there is covered with thick clouds and Death flaps its wings above the path."

Christian said, "From all that you have told me, it is clear that this is the path I must take if I am to reach my goal."

"It may be your path," said the two cowards. "It is certainly not ours."

And with that they turned and ran, leaving Christian to walk by himself into the perils from which they had fled.

As it threaded its way along the valley, the track grew narrower and narrower. To the right yawned a ditch, so deep that Christian could not see to the bottom. Into that ditch blind fools have led other fools for thousands of years. All have died miserably in its depths.

To the left of the track spread a quagmire, stinking of brackish water. Its surface looked firm and solid, but anyone who set foot there soon found himself struggling in choking, black mud. Even a good man, once in the grip of this bog, could find no solid ground on which to save himself from a horrible death.

To make matters worse, the air was growing darker and darker. Christian did not know whether night was falling or whether it was because of the clouds overhanging the valley. He sighed, overcome with the difficulties which faced him. If he kept to the left-hand side of the path, he was safe from the ditch, but might easily stumble into the quagmire. If he moved too far to the right, he would be sure to slip over the edge of the ditch and tumble to his death down its steep slope. He could not see far enough in front of him to know where he was setting his feet on the uneven surface of the track.

As he struggled on, Christian smelt smoke. It was not

the pleasant smell of burning wood, but a foul, raw stench, unlike anything he had smelt before. He began to cough and splutter and his mouth filled with a bitter taste. A dull red light began to glow alongside the path and sparks rained about the pilgrim's head, threatening to blind him or set fire to his hair. Violent sounds rang in his ears—the splitting of huge rocks, the hiss of escaping gases, and the roar of leaping flames.

This was the Mouth of Hell. Against its dangers Christian's sword offered no protection.

"Lord," he cried, "keep me safe from the perils that surround me!"

As he spoke a great tongue of fire licked across the path. Pitch-black smoke billowed around, and there was a sound of rushing feet, as if a herd of maddened bulls were stampeding along the track. Christian did not know what would become of him—whether he would be burnt alive, smothered, or trampled into the ground.

"I am almost ready to turn and run," he said. "But I have come so far that it may well be safer to press on. Besides, I have not lost courage in all the dangers I have faced so far. So I will walk bravely forward, come what may!"

Again he heard the sound of rushing feet. He saw now that the flames were full of demons and monsters, who scampered across in front of him, uttering hideous yells.

"I will fare onward!" cried Christian. "Give way, for I walk in the strength of the Lord!"

At this, the fiends retreated, and for the rest of the journey they did not dare approach him.

But a new torment awaited Christian, in some ways more terrible than anything he had yet endured. As he went on, he began to hear a voice speaking ill of the Lord, saying that his power was nothing but a dream.

"It is all a trick," said the mocking voice. "The Lord, in whom you place such trust, is no better than the Devil. He has led you into this place of darkness and here he means to make an end of you."

In his confusion, Christian felt sure that it was his own voice that he heard. He was miserable to think that he could be saying such things, but still the voice whispered in his ears. Tears of regret and anger filled his eyes.

The darkness had by now grown so thick that Christian could not see his hand when he held it up to his face. This was the worst part of his journey. He thought that death was the only release from his misery and his heart was desolate and empty.

Suddenly a clear voice rang out ahead of him, saying: *"Though I walk through the Valley of the Shadow of Death, I will fear no harm, for the Lord is with me."*

When he heard these words of comfort, Christian was overcome with relief.

"Then I am not the only servant of the Lord walking through this dreadful place!" he cried. "Although I cannot see him, he is with me, and will give me strength. I have only to hurry on my way, and I shall meet other pilgrims, and need travel alone no longer."

By and by the darkness grew less. The sun's rays slanted down into the valley and he could see where he was going. He looked back at the path he had been following and realized that to have come so far was a miracle. He saw how narrow the track was, how the ditch and the quagmire stretched along its sides. He saw goblins and hobgoblins, goat-men and dragons; but they were in the distance now. In the light of day he could look at them without fear.

The rest of his journey was at least as dangerous as the part he had already travelled. The path was full of ruts

and pitfalls, deep, black holes where a man could easily
break his neck. Snares and traps were lying in wait for
the unwary. If he had had to walk here in the darkness,
Christian would surely have perished, even if he had had
a thousand lives. But it was broad day now, and he
made his way cautiously out of the Valley of the Shadow
of Death.

He now had to cross an open space which was covered
with blood and ashes. Mangled bodies lay where they
had fallen and white skeletons shone horribly in the
sunlight.

"These must be the corpses of poor pilgrims who have
passed by here before me," thought Christian. "I wonder
what man or beast put them to death in such a cruel
way?"

The answer was not hard to find. Beside the path were
the entrances to two caves, the dwelling-places of giants
in the olden days. These giants, called Pope and Pagan,
had been pitiless enemies to all who travelled past their
door. It was their wicked power which had caused the
death of the pilgrims whose bodies lay on the track.

But they did not harm Christian. Pagan had died long
ago, and men went in fear of him no more. Pope was
still alive, but he had grown so old, so stiff in his limbs
and feeble in his wits that it was no very hard task to
avoid him. He sat in the mouth of his cave, grinning like
an idiot, and did not notice Christian until he had almost
gone past.

Then indeed he did rouse himself for a moment,
shaking his fist and threatening to burn Christian alive.
But the pilgrim took very little notice of him, keeping his
eyes on the path and walking on quite unharmed. He
soon found himself climbing a gentle slope. When he had
reached the top, he saw a sight which put fresh courage

into his weary heart. His friend Faithful, his neighbour in the town of Destruction and now his fellow pilgrim, was walking briskly along the path some way ahead.

"Ho-ho!" cried Christian. "Ho-ho! Faithful! Wait for me to catch up with you, and I will be your companion."

9

Faithful's Story

Christian began to run along the path, calling out to his friend to wait for him. Faithful did not pause, but looked over his shoulder and cried out, "No, I cannot wait, I am running for my life, and all my enemies are behind me."

Christian understood that Faithful was in a great hurry to reach the safety of Zion. He put on a burst of speed and managed to overtake his friend.

"Look," he said. "I've got in front of you now!"

As he was boasting of his success, his foot caught on a rock and he fell sprawling in the dust. At this the two pilgrims burst out laughing. Faithful gave his arm to Christian and helped him to his feet. Then they walked on together, talking as old friends do.

At first they spoke chiefly of what had happened in the City of Destruction.

"I thought I would be able to travel with you the whole way," said Faithful, "but you had the start of me."

"How long did you stay after I had left?" asked Christian.

"Soon after you went, everyone began to speak of the fire from Heaven which was sure to burn up every house in the town. I waited no longer, but set off to find safety."

"But if everyone was talking about the fire, why didn't they all escape with you?"

"Everyone was talking about it," replied Faithful, "but if you ask me most of them didn't believe what they were saying. Although you had made your escape, they spoke of you as a fool. However, I knew that the fire would indeed descend upon us, so I followed in your footsteps."

Christian asked what had become of Pliable, the neighbour who had come with him on the first stage of his journey.

"He came back covered with mud, and we knew that he must have fallen into the Slough of Despond. He denies it, but everyone mocks him for his feeble courage. Hang him, they say, he's a turncoat. They laugh at him in the street, and he's seven times worse off than if he'd never left the city in the first place."

"I had hopes of that man," said Christian. "But now I can see that he'll perish with the rest of them when the city is destroyed. He's like the old pig—you can wash him as clean as you like, but he'll soon be wallowing in the filth and slime again."

"I'm afraid you're right," said Faithful. "What can we do, though?"

"There are some people beyond our help," agreed Christian. "Let's forget Destruction and its inhabitants, and talk about our own fortunes since we set out. Come, tell me of your adventures—for I'm sure you must have met with many."

As they walked together, Faithful told his friend of the dangers he had faced in his journey. He told him of the beautiful Wanton, of old Adam the First, of grumbling Discontent and of cunning Shame—all tempters who had tried to turn Faithful's steps and prevent him from reaching the Eternal City.

"I kept clear of the Slough," began Faithful, "and got through the little gate without difficulty. Soon after that I

70

met with Wanton. She was the most beautiful woman I
had ever seen; when she spoke to me, she fixed her eyes
on mine until I could feel my brain spinning. She told me
that I had only to go with her and I would be granted
all my wishes."

"Thank God you did not turn aside!" cried Christian.
"She has been the ruin of hundreds."

"I shut my eyes, so I would not be tempted by her
beauty, and went on my way. It was a hard struggle, but
I escaped. However, a second tempter soon appeared. I
was at the foot of that steep hill called Difficulty, when
he came up and asked who I was. He was bent with age,
and his name was Adam the First.

"'You look like an honest fellow,' he said. 'I pay good
wages, and if you want to stay on and work for me I'll
willingly find you a job.'

"I asked him to tell me a little more about where he
lived, what kind of household his was, and what wages he
paid.

"'I live in the town of Deceit,' he said. 'Nothing's
lacking in my house—all the dainty foods of the world
are spread on my table, my servants wait on me hand
and foot. I've got three children already—but if you want
to work for me, I'll make you my heir, and you will
inherit all my riches.'"

"And did you go with this man?" asked Christian.

"I was tempted for a while," said Faithful. "Something
about him put me off, however. He seemed to be just the
kind of person I was running from. Then I had a sudden
teror that if I went with him he would sell me as a slave.
I told him to hold his tongue, for I had no intention of
going to his house. He flew into a rage and began to
curse me, saying that he would send someone after me to
make my journey miserable. He pinched my flesh in his

gnarled old hands, but he could not hold me, and I ran off up the hill."

"And did he send anyone after you?"

"Do you remember a green meadow and a wooden seat?" asked Faithful.

"I do," said Christian. "It was there that I fell asleep and lost my scroll."

"As I crossed that clearing," continued Faithful, "a man came running up behind me."

" 'Take that!' he shouted as soon as he had drawn level with me, and he dealt me a mighty blow which laid me flat on my back.

"When I had recovered my senses, I asked him what I had done wrong.

" 'You stopped and talked with old Adam,' he replied. 'You were even tempted to go with him. I have come to punish you.' And so saying he gave me another blow which knocked the breath out of my body.

"I began to cry out for mercy, but he said that he had never heard of mercy. He went on hitting me blow after blow until I thought my end had come."

"How did you escape from him?" asked Christian. "Did someone come to your rescue?"

"Our Lord came and saved me," said Faithful. "I recognized him by the marks on his body, which he received on the cross. He told the bully to spare me and leave me to get on with my journey. So I made my way out of the clearing and went on up the hill."

"The man who beat you was Moses," said Christian. "He's a merciless fellow. If anyone breaks his laws, he has no pity for them."

"I recognized him," replied Faithful. "He's the man who came to me when I was living in Destruction, and told me my house was going to be burnt to ashes."

"When you reached the top of the hill, you must have passed by the Palace Beautiful," said Christian. "The porter told me that he had seen you. It's a pity you didn't stop there, for the place is full of rare marvels."

"It was early in the day when I arrived," explained Faithful. "I thought I had better continue my journey. The lions at the gate must have been sleeping, for they gave me no trouble. I went on down the other side of the mountain, and soon found myself in the Valley of Humiliation. It was there that I met with Discontent."

"And he, too, wanted you to give up your pilgrimage?"

"Yes, he said that there was nothing to be gained by travelling through the valley.

"'If you take this path,' he said, 'your friends and relations—people like Pride and Worldly Glory—will call you a fool.'

"I had my answer ready. I told him that these people might be related to me by blood, but I had turned my back on them and their ways, and they were nothing to me now.

"'Besides,' I said, 'this may be the Valley of Humiliation, but through it runs the way to the greatest glory of all.'"

"And the last enemy you met with was Shame," said Christian. "Tell me about him. Was he a difficult opponent to overcome?"

"He sneered at religion and all who were interested in it," replied Faithful.

"'It's a pitiful, low, sneaking business,' he said, 'to be always forgiving and asking for forgiveness. A man shouldn't be ashamed of sticking up for himself. How many rich and powerful men do you find reading the Bible? They've got more sense than to sit listening to dreary sermons and then crawl whining home afterwards.'

" 'What kind of people are these pilgrims?' he asked. 'Miserable paupers, half of them, without the faintest idea of science. They can't mix with people of wealth and fashion, so they go sneaking off on their pilgrimages. But any man of sense would have too much shame to be seen with them.'

"At first I blushed to listen to him," admitted Faithful, "and could not think how to answer. Then it struck me that he had been full of talk of the world, but had said nothing of the Lord.

" 'Sir,' I said to him, 'we all know that those things which men hold in great respect may be worth nothing to God. Remember this: a poor man who loves Christ is richer by far than a wealthy merchant who despises him. Get you gone, for I see that you wish to hinder me from reaching my goal, and I have no more patience with you.' "

"Did he leave you alone after that?" asked Christian.

"Well, he followed me some way further, whispering in my ear and trying to change my mind. In the end, though, he gave up, for he saw that he had no hope of success."

"I am glad you escaped from this villain," said Christian. "Was the rest of your journey as hard as the part you have told me about?"

"No, I was lucky enough to have glorious sunshine from that moment onwards. All through the Valley of the Shadow of Death my path was plain to see, and I travelled it without meeting a single danger."

Christian looked at his friend and smiled.

"You certainly *were* lucky," he said. "In the Valley of Humiliation I had to do battle with the terrible Apollyon, the fiend with the mouth of a lion. He had me down in the dust, and I thought my last hour had come. But by the help of God I grasped my sword and plunged it into his belly.

"Then I came to the Valley of the Shadow of Death, and while I was there it was black night for half the journey. I never thought I would get out at the other end. However, day broke at last, and my path grew easier.

"And now I have caught up with you, Faithful, my friend, and we can continue our pilgrimage together."

10

The Talkative Pilgrim

Christian and Faithful went on their way in good spirits. The path was wide here, and the journey was easy. After a while, a third pilgrim came abreast of them, a tall man who had seemed handsome enough at a distance, but whose face was not so attractive at close quarters.

"Where are you going, my friend?" Faithful asked the stranger. "Are you planning to travel to the Holy City?"

"Indeed I am," said the third pilgrim, "and I will be happy to be your companion on the way."

"Very well, let us go together. We can pass the time in serious conversation."

When Faithful said this, the stranger, whose name was Talkative, took his hand and shook it with great earnestness.

"My friend," he said, "nothing pleases me more than to talk seriously, with you or with anyone else. How glad I am that I have found someone who shares my taste! These days the roads are filled with idle chatterers whose talk is nothing but gossip and vanity."

Christian had been listening to these words with a slight smile on his face. When he heard this speech of Talkative's, he dropped back a little so that he could overhear what was said without taking any part in the conversation.

"Ahh!" said Talkative. "Nothing can give me more pleasure than to talk about God and his miracles. If you have any interest in the miraculous, where can you find such splendid stories as are told in the Bible?"

"That's true, of course," agreed Faithful. "But when we speak of these matters, it shouldn't be just for the sake of entertainment. We should aim to learn from our conversations, so they will be useful to us, and not simply a way of passing time."

"Oh, yes, yes, I'm with you there. But it's almost bound to be useful to talk of heavenly things. Think of the knowledge you gain! You learn about the unimportance of worldly affairs, and the higher glory of the world that is to come. By talking, you can learn how to repent, how to pray, how to suffer, how to teach the ignorant. You can discuss the promises contained in the Gospels, and be comforted by thinking of the good fortune which awaits you. By talking to your friends, you can come to realize the uselessness of human effort, and this will mean that you no longer strive to do anything. You simply discuss with your acquaintances—there is nothing more to be done ..."

Faithful began to lose patience with Talkative. He seemed to think that everything was a question of mere words. What was more, he didn't even talk about anything in particular: he opened his mouth and out came a flood of fine words.

"Well, my friend," he said. "What shall we take as our topic for the present?"

"Anything you like!" replied Talkative. "Heavenly things or earthly things; things of the past or things of the future; human morality or the state of the Church; sacred or profane matters; things foreign or at home."

When he heard this great list of subjects, Faithful's doubts grew. He slowed his pace a little, allowing Christian to catch up with him.

"This new companion of ours seems to be a splendid fellow," he whispered. "Don't you agree?"

Christian smiled gently when he heard this. "This new friend of yours, Faithful, will take in twenty simpletons with his smooth tongue before so much as one man sees through him."

"Do you know him, then?" asked Faithful.

"Know him! I know him better than he knows himself. I'm surprised you haven't recognized him, for he lives in our town. He is Talkative, the son of Say-Well, and lives in Prating Row, and I can tell you that for all his fine tongue he's nothing but a rogue."

"Well, you can't deny that he's a very good-looking man," said Faithful.

"True," said Christian, "provided you don't look too close! He reminds me of those paintings that seem so fine from a few yards off. When you walk up to them, you see a very different sight."

"You smiled as you said that," said Faithful, "so I suppose you are only joking."

"God forbid!" said Christian earnestly. "You know I would never accuse a man falsely, even in jest. No, let me tell you more about this Talkative. He's one of those chaps who always have a word in their mouths, no matter where they find themselves. Put him down at a table in an ale-house, and he'd be prattling on just as he was to you. The drunker he got, too, the more his talk would be filled with holy words. True religion has no place in his heart, or his house, or his behaviour; all his faith is in his tongue, and what he likes best is to set that tongue wagging."

"Although I was uncertain, I believed that he was a good man," said Faithful. "I see now that I was sadly taken in."

"You surely were! Remember this proverb: they speak, and do nothing; but the Kingdom of God is not in words, but in the power to act. This man Talkative is forever speaking of Prayer, of Repentance, of the New Birth; but he does no more than speak of them. I have visited his family; I have watched his behaviour both at home and around the town. You may be sure that when I tell you about him, I am telling the truth. And the truth is this: his life has as much religion in it as the white of an egg has flavour!

"The townspeople—those of them that know him—have a saying which describes him well. They call him 'a Saint in public and a Devil at home'. For his private life is as sinful as his talk is full of pretended goodness. His wicked ways have been the ruin of many poor folk; and they will be the ruin of many more, unless God puts an end to his villainy.

"What is more, he has been the shame of religion in our town. Nobody speaks more loudly or more often of God, of virtue, of holiness. The townsfolk compare his words with his deeds; and the result is that they no longer believe any other man who speaks of the Lord! For they think all religious speakers are as deceitful as this hypocrite Talkative."

"I'm sure that you're not saying these things out of ill will," said Faithful, "so I am bound to believe you."

"I might have been taken in myself," admitted Christian, "if I hadn't known him of old. But I assure you he's a wretch whom no good man will own as a friend."

"It's clear, then," said Faithful, "that saying and doing are two separate things. From now on, I shall bear this in mind."

"They are indeed separate things—as different as the soul and the body. The body without a soul is no more than a carcass, and words without deeds are likewise worthless. The soul of religion is in action—in visiting widows and orphans, and in keeping clear of all sin. Talkative doesn't realise this; but when the time comes for us to be judged, it is deeds that will count, and all his long sentences will be of no help to him then."

Faithful sighed. "However I may have liked his company at first, I am sick of it now," he said. "But how are we to be rid of this man?"

"If you take my advice," said Christian, "you will begin a conversation with him, just as you have promised to do. Ask him about the power of religion. When he tells you how he believes in that power—as he certainly will—ask him whether any trace of it is to be found in his heart, his household, or his behaviour."

Faithful lengthened his stride until he was once again level with the third pilgrim.

"How are you, my friend?" he asked.

"Well," said Talkative, "I must say I'd hoped we would have begun our conversation by now."

"Very well, let us begin. I thought you might like to explain to me what happens to a man when the power of religion enters into his heart."

Talkative frowned, as if he were thinking this over. "A good question," he said. "A very good question ..."

"Come," said Faithful. "Your answer, my friend?"

"The first sign is that a man, once religion is in his heart, begins to cry out against sin."

"In my opinion, it is not crying out that matters. The important thing is that a man should no longer do any sinful deeds."

"I don't see the difference," said Talkative.

"Some folks cry out against sin just as a mother scolds her child," explained Faithful. "One minute they are in a rage with it, but the next they are nursing and encouraging it again."

"You're trying to catch me out!" said Talkative.

"No, no, I'm simply trying to get at the truth. Come, tell me your second sign."

Talkative said that the second sign was that a man knew the Bible in great detail.

"Knowledge by itself is nothing," said Faithful. "Have you never met a man who knew exactly what his master wanted of him, and yet failed to perform it? Knowledge is nothing, as I say, unless it is the true knowledge which shows itself in willingness to act."

At this Talkative flew into a rage. When Faithful asked him for a third sign, he refused to speak, saying that they would never agree on anything.

"In that case," said Faithful, "let me tell you something. If a man is truly full of religion, it will be obvious to himself and to those who meet him. He will have confessed his faith in Christ, and his life will show that his faith is real. His heart will be holy, the life of his family will be holy, and his behaviour in the world will be holy. Answer this question, Talkative. Have you such faith, and is your life holy, as it should be if you have?"

Talkative began to blush and stammer. "This is not at all the kind of discussion I was thinking of," he complained. "Do you think you are a judge? Why are you asking me these questions?"

"When I met you," replied Faithful, "I noticed how keen you were to talk, and I wondered if you had anything else apart from your ready tongue. To tell the truth, I have heard that you are one of those whose religion lies in their mouths, and whose behaviour is a disgrace to true Christianity."

At this, Talkative lost his temper once again. "If you're

the kind who listens to all the gossip which goes around, then I have no more to say to you!" he shouted. And with an angry scowl he turned his back and marched away.

Christian came up to his friend. "I knew how it would be. Rather than change his way of living, Talkative has chosen to leave your company. He is gone, I am happy to say, for I would much rather continue our journey without him."

"I am glad I spoke to him," said Faithful. "Now he has at least had the chance to think about his way of life. If he goes on in the old style, it won't be our fault."

"It is always best to be blunt with fellows like him," said Christian. "That way, at least they have something to think about, but if you listen calmly to them and never disagree they go on their way without a doubt in the world as to their own rightness."

The pilgrims were now walking through a barren wilderness, where few plants grew and nothing refreshed their weary eyes. However, they had plenty to talk about, and the journey was never dull.

Eventually they reached the edge of this wild country, and Faithful stopped to look back at the path they had travelled.

"See!" he cried. "There is someone following us. Who is it, Christian?"

When Christian recognized the distant figure, his heart leapt with joy. It was his old friend Evangelist, the man who had helped him in his first attempts to leave Destruction and set out on his pilgrimage to the Heavenly City.

II

At Vanity Fair

"Greetings, my dear friends!" cried Evangelist as he drew level with the two pilgrims. "May peace be with you, and those who help you."

Christian and Faithful embraced him warmly, telling him how delightful it was to see the face of such a trusty friend after the long and perilous journey they had made.

As they walked, the travellers told Evangelist of the trials they had faced, the temptations that had attacked them and the monsters they had overcome. When they had come to the end of their stories, he sighed and said he was sorry they had had to cope with such dangers and difficulties.

"But how glad I am that you have won the victory!" he said. "The time is coming when you will reap the reward of all your toil. Before you a crown of gold is set, a crown that will never rust and whose brightness will never fade. This crown is yours, if you can only hold out. Keep all your thoughts on the Kingdom of Heaven; do not be distracted by the doings of this world. Concentrate on your goal and set your faces as hard as flint against the lures of wickedness. Hold out, and the crown is yours."

When Christian and Faithful heard these stirring words, their hearts glowed with determination.

"You can help us on our way," said Christian. "What you have just said fills us with courage, and we thank you for that courage. But you can do more than that. We know that you have the power of foreseeing the future. You can tell us of fresh enemies lying in wait, and explain how best to overcome them. You can foretell all that will befall us from now to our journey's end."

Evangelist frowned. He could not at first make up his mind to answer Christian's question.

"Come," said Faithful. "Tell us what lies in wait for us. Whatever it may be, we have strength to bear it."

"My sons," said Evangelist, "you know already that the road you have chosen is not an easy one. You have met troubles and torments enough since you left the City of Destruction, and it will not surprise you when I say that there are more trials in store.

"We are almost out of this wilderness, as you can see. Before long you will find yourselves in a busy town. There you will be surrounded by foes, who will do their best to put you both to death. At least one of you will not leave that town alive; and perhaps you will both die there."

Christian and Faithful looked at one another in fear. So far they had conquered their enemies; but this time it seemed that they would fail.

"Be sure of this," said Evangelist, "and do not give way to despair. Whoever dies in this city will die unnaturally, and perhaps painfully too. But he will be the lucky one, luckier than his companion. So long as he holds fast to his faith, he will soon dwell in the Holy City while his friend is still struggling with the perils of the journey. Be faithful unto death, and the Lord will give you a crown of life."

So saying, Evangelist took leave of his friends, clasping their hands firmly and wishing them strength and courage for the pilgrimage. Christian and Faithful walked on in

silence until they came to the outskirts of a large and
bustling town.

Alleys led off to right and left, each thronged with
people. Tall buildings rose high on all sides blocking the
sky and casting deep shadows everywhere. Beneath striped
awnings salesmen stood shouting, calling out in praise of
their wares and encouraging the crowds to buy.

"This must be the weekly market," said Christian to
his friend. "What a din! I don't think I've ever seen
such crowds of people, or such heaps of merchandise."

A man wheeling a barrow shot out from a side-street,
almost knocking Faithful off his feet. He was about to
rush off again, but Faithful called out to him.

"Friend! Wait a moment. Can you tell us the name of
this place?"

"Vanity," said the man. "Surely you have heard of the
famous town of Vanity?"

"And this must be the weekly fair, I suppose?"

"Weekly fair!" said the man scornfully. "It isn't weekly,
nor monthly neither, I can tell you. It's Vanity Fair, the
greatest in the world, and it never stops, rain or shine,
working-day or holiday."

The man seized the shafts of his barrow and hurried
on his way.

This fair, into which the pilgrims had wandered, was
no recent fashion. It had been going on for thousands of
years, and its founder was the Devil himself. He had
noticed that the way of all pilgrims lay through this town
of Vanity, and had set up a market here in which all the
bright goods of the world were on show. There was
nothing a man could not buy in these crowded streets:
houses and lands, pleasures and delights of all sorts, silver
and gold and sparkling jewels—everything was for sale.
There was something from every country in the world:

rich sweets from Persia, gaudy silks from the East, African ivory, heavy furs from the far north. Each country had its own street: Faithful and Christian saw signs saying Spanish Row, French Street, and Italian Court.

There were sideshows in every square—puppet theatres, jugglers, and conjurors. Idle folk stood gawking at the spectacle, their mouths wide with foolish wonder. But the pilgrims never paused, for their goal was the Eternal City, and they had no time to waste in arriving there. They knew that the Lord himself, the Prince of Princes, had come through this same Fair on his way to Zion. The Devil had tempted him, leading him from street to street and showing him all the riches of the world. But he had not spent one farthing in the town, and had refused to give the Devil any sign of respect.

As the pilgrims passed through the Fair, they caused a great commotion. The idlers in the streets gazed at them and made puzzled comments on their strange appearance and manner.

"Have you seen these two? Look at the clothes they're wearing!"

"If you ask me," said one narrow-faced woman, "they're a couple of madmen escaped from Bedlam. We ought to take them back and have them locked up again."

"I can't understand a word they say," said a third voice. "Must be some foreign tongue. Pair of savages, perhaps!"

What caused the greatest astonishment was the pilgrims' refusal to look at the piles of fine wares which lay all around them. If any stallholder called out to them, egging them on to buy, they would put their fingers in their ears and look up to Heaven, saying that they had no wish to see the wares of Vanity.

Finally one man leapt out from behind his stall and

laid hold of Christian's shoulder, forcing him to stop.

"Look here," he said. "You don't want this, and you don't want that. Whatever we show you, you turn up your noses. Well, answer me one question. What *do* you want to buy?"

Christian and Faithful, with serious faces, replied with one voice, "We will buy the truth."

At this there was a great hoot of laughter and the noise and shouting grew twice as loud. The pilgrims were surrounded by a crowd of scornful townspeople, eager to put them to shame. The hubbub became so violent that the Ruler of this wicked town appeared on the scene. He saw at once that the two strangers were the cause of the trouble, and sent his henchmen into the crowd to arrest them.

"Grab hold of them," he ordered, "and bring them to me. We'll have to ask these two fine fellows a few questions. Then, unless they can find some good excuses, we'll lock them up, and put an end to their mischief-making."

12

Christian and Faithful Imprisoned

At first Christian and Faithful were relieved when they saw half a dozen armed men pushing through the crowd towards them.

"Perhaps they are coming to take us to a safe place where we will not have to listen to shouts and insults," said Christian.

But when the men reached the pilgrims, they seized them roughly by the arms and, without saying a word, dragged them through the throng of people and led them off through a maze of narrow streets. They were taken into a tall dingy building and made to sit in a large room. After some time the Ruler of the city appeared with a number of his friends. At once they began to fire questions at the travellers, scarcely giving them time to answer.

"Where do you come from?"

"Where are you going? What are you doing in this town?"

"Why do you wear such unusual clothes?"

Christian and Faithful did their best to explain that they were citizens of Destruction who had nothing more to do with the world, but were intent on arriving in the Heavenly City.

"And how did you come to be the cause of such a hullabaloo?" asked the Ruler, staring at their faces with his cruel eyes.

"We did nothing to provoke the tradespeople," said Christian. "I don't know why they began to insult us and tried to block our path. There is only one explanation I can think of. One man asked us angrily what we wanted to buy and we answered him truly that the truth was the only thing we wanted."

At this the questioners looked knowingly at one another, and began to whisper among themselves.

"A couple of lunatics," said one.

"Quite," agreed a second man. "It's obvious that we should lock them up—make an example of them."

Christian and Faithful were marched away into another room. Here they were beaten by the guards and their faces and bodies rubbed with filth. A metal cage was set up in the chief square. The two pilgrims were locked up in it so that all day long they were mocked and threatened by passers-by. If any of the townspeople felt spiteful or ill-tempered, all their hatred could be poured out on the strangers in the cage.

Several people pretended that the pilgrims were animals, and offered them food through the iron bars of their prison.

The Ruler of the City came every day to watch. It always brought a savage smile to his face to see how Christian and his companion were tormented.

But however harshly they were treated, the pilgrims never lost their calm temper. If someone spoke to them with especial brutality, they were especially gentle in their replies. To a flood of curses they returned blessings and good wishes. If some ruffian hurled a stone at them, they did not throw it back but prayed that he might get the better of his wicked nature.

The people noticed their good humour and patience and some were led to speak out in their favour.

"If they're such a pair of villains and madmen, why do they bear our insults so calmly?" an old woman said one day.

"Yes," agreed her neighbour. "We should leave them in peace. They're locked up as it is. That's punishment enough, isn't it, friends? Why should we make their lives more miserable by our cruelty?"

But not everyone was so kind. Most of the citizens continued to abuse the pilgrims and would hear nothing in their favour. Talk of treating them less harshly filled these people with scorn.

"Oh yes, be merciful to them, you say, do you? If you want to be friends, why don't you join them in their cage? There's room for a couple more if you squeeze up a bit!"

At this the old woman came to their defence. "I know one thing," she said. "There are plenty of folk walking the streets this morning who *do* deserve to be locked up! Whatever these two may have done wrong, I can point to a good few villains worse than either of them, living in Vanity Fair."

The argument grew fiercer and fiercer, though Christian and Faithful took care to remain quiet and do nothing to encourage the citizens in their anger. At length two men came to blows in front of their cage. The fight seemed likely to spread; soon there would be a riot in the streets. When he saw trouble brewing, the Ruler again sent his guards into the square to take the prisoners from their cage and bring them before him.

"Even when you are locked in a cage, you fill the town with violence!" he shouted. "This latest trouble is all because of you. We have been too soft. This time your punishment will be more severe."

The pilgrims were led away by the guards and beaten

even more brutally than before. Then they were put into great iron chains which clanked with every step they took. Heavy weights were hung upon them. In this pitiful state they were marched out into the streets and made to walk up and down in front of the townsfolk while the guards pointed them out as an example to wrongdoers.

"Anyone else want to speak out in favour of these two?" said the chief guard, a surly, brutal wretch. "If you do, this is how you'll end up—dragging your chains about the market-place."

Still the two companions bore their misfortunes patiently. They spoke gently even to the guards who so cruelly maltreated them. Nothing could move them to a rage, and nothing could stop them praying for the very people who caused them the greatest pain.

Once more a number of citizens began to feel sorry for them, and to say that their treatment was too harsh. Their calm endurance filled many with admiration, and even though few were willing to speak out openly on their behalf, whispers of sympathy were heard in every street. But for the most part the inhabitants of Vanity were solidly against the strangers, and when they discovered that people were taking their side again, they grew angrier than ever.

"We have tried the cage, and we have tried chains and weights," said the chief guard. "Neither has done any good. We must put these two pilgrims to death, or there will be no end to the trouble they will cause."

"Very well," said the Ruler of the city. "We shall put them on trial. In a week's time the case will be heard and if they are found guilty they must pay with their lives. Meanwhile, they are to be returned to the cage and must remain imprisoned in the square until the day of the trial."

So the pilgrims were locked in the cage and their feet were made fast in the stocks. Every passer-by was free to spit on them, to mock them and to torment them with threats of their coming death. It was a long week for the two friends, but they comforted each other in their distress, and their friendship made misfortune more bearable.

"Evangelist warned us that we would be surrounded by enemies in this place," said Faithful. "His prophecy has come true. But we should not forget that whoever dies at the hands of these wicked men will travel at once to the City of Zion. For him the trials of the journey will be over."

"I know," said Christian. "Let's not despair. As you say, when one of us is put to death, it will only shorten his travels."

Secretly each pilgrim wished that he might be the one to be killed in Vanity. But they said nothing of this, being content to leave the decision to the Lord. Meanwhile they kept their spirits high by thinking that the crown of life was theirs, if they only kept faith to the end.

When the week was over, the two prisoners were led to the courtroom. They were weak from hunger and ill-treatment, their clothes were tattered, and their skins were dark with grime. They were a pathetic sight when the guards marched them up the middle of the hall and stood them in the dock. The Judge, whose name was Lord Hate-good, sneered down at them from his bench while the charge against them was read in a flat, heavy voice.

"These men are accused of being disturbers of trade in our city, and causers of commotions and disturbances. They are further accused of having stirred up the people in their favour, and of having so created a division of opinion in the town which is a danger to peace. All this is in contradiction to the law and in contempt of its power."

Faithful was to be tried before Christian, and he now began to speak in his own defence.

"If I have made an enemy of any man," he said, "it is because that man himself is the enemy of the Lord. As for disturbance, I am a man of peace, and nobody quarrels at my wish. If any of the people spoke in our favour, that is because they were won over by our truth and our innocence. Finally, as for your Ruler, he is none other than the Devil, the Prince of Darkness. I defy him and all his helpers!"

Faithful's bold words rang out in the courtroom, but the hard face of the Judge was unmoved. He did not speak to the pilgrim, but issued a proclamation to the citizens. This stated that if any person wished to speak against the prisoners, he should come forward. As the judge's voice died away, three men sprang eagerly to their feet and began to push their way forward to the front of the hall.

You had only to look at these men to recognize that they were three of the wickedest wretches who ever walked the earth. Their names were Envy, Superstition and Pickthank, and they were in a great hurry to give evidence against Faithful, for it was their dearest wish to cause the good pilgrim's death.

13

The Trial and Death of Faithful

Envy was the first of the three wicked witnesses to give evidence against Faithful. He strode up the middle of the courtroom, turned to the Judge and at once began to deliver his hateful speech.

"My Lord," he said, "I have known this man a long time, and I will swear before you all that——"

"Wait, wait!" cried the Judge. "Before I can hear your evidence, you must take the oath."

Although Envy was full of lies and malice, he placed his hand on the Bible and promised that what he was about to say was the truth, the whole truth and nothing but the truth.

"My Lord," he continued, "this man, although he has the fine name of Faithful, is one of the vilest men in the whole country. A good citizen—a fellow like myself— is content with the law of the land, and so long as he respects the Prince and his officers, he deserves to be left in peace. But this man Faithful is forever trying to fill people's heads with his fine notions of faith and holiness. I myself have heard him say that the laws of our town of Vanity were the exact opposite of the commandments of Christianity. In his opinion, all our excellent customs are worth less than nothing! That's the kind of trouble-maker he is, Sir."

The Judge asked Envy if he had anything to add.

"There's plenty more I could say, only I'm afraid I might begin to bore the Court, your Honour. Why not let these two gentlemen have their say? But if you need a bit more evidence before you can put this wretch to death, I'll be happy to do what I can when the time comes."

"Thank you, my man," said the Judge. "The next witness, I believe, is Superstition. If you would like to come to the witness-box, Superstition, we look forward to hearing what you can tell us."

"I don't know the man very well," began the second witness. "However, the other day I happened to overhear a snatch of his conversation, and that was enough for me to know what kind of fellow he was. He was speaking about the religion of our town, and saying that it had no value in the eyes of God—why, he said as much to me when I spoke to him myself.

"I needn't tell you what that means, your Honour. This man Faithful actually believes that the folk of this noble town are a crowd of sinners and that we'll all go to Hell when we die!"

When Superstition said these words, there was a murmur of anger from the assembly. The Judge gave Faithful a brief glance as if to say, "We will soon make an end of you, my friend!" Then he called forth Pickthank, the third witness.

Pickthank was a miserable, snivelling little man, and as he shambled up the aisle, his bloodshot eyes shone with hatred.

"This man has spoken ill of our noble Prince Beelzebub," he began. "Not only that, he has shown his scorn of all the fine Lords of Vanity. I have heard him mock them in public—Sir Having Greedy, Lord Luxurious, Lord Desire of Vain Glory—and many others beside. He said that if he could persuade the citizens to his point of view, not one of these noblemen would be allowed to remain in the town.

"You yourself, my Lord Hate-good, have been the object of his vile attacks. With my own ears I heard him call you an ungodly villain!"

Pickthank was dismissed, and the Judge turned to the prisoner.

"Faithful, you treacherous heretic!" he shouted in a voice trembling with rage. "Have you heard what these three gentlemen have said about you?"

"May I speak a few words in my own defence?" replied Faithful.

"You deserve to die this very instant!" said Lord Hate-good. "However, I'm no tyrant, and to show everyone that I know how to be merciful, I'm prepared to let you speak."

"As to what Envy said against me," began Faithful, "all I said was that if a law or custom is against the will of God, it must be against Christianity. To Superstition's evidence, I reply that whatever religion is invented by men, it cannot be the same as the true religion revealed by God.

"Pickthank has told you that I publicly attacked the nobility of this town, and I will not deny his story. For what I said is nothing less than the truth. Prince Beelzebub, the Ruler of Vanity, is the Devil himself, and every one of his attendants is fit for Hell. I have spoken; may the Lord have mercy on me."

Again a murmur of astonishment ran round the hall. Faithful's boldness and plain speaking were breathtaking.

Lord Hate-good called for silence and turned to address the jury.

"Gentlemen of the jury," he began, "here is this man who has created such an uproar in our town. You have heard what has been spoken against him by the honourable witnesses. It is now up to you to spare or condemn him. Before you begin your discussion, I must remind you of the law.

"Long ago, in the time of Pharaoh, it was decreed that any man who left the religion of Vanity should be thrown into the river. It was the same in the days of Nebuchadnezzar the Great: either men knelt before his golden image, or they were flung into the fiery furnace. Darius, too, insisted that men should worship as he ordered, and if they did not, why, they were given to the lions, who made short work of them!

"This man, this wretched Faithful, has not only refused to bow down to our Prince—he has encouraged others to follow his wicked example. His own words condemn him. It is clear that he is a hardened criminal against our laws, and deserves to die for his treason."

When the Judge had finished advising them, the jury retired into another room. They were a collection of rogues, as their names showed. Mr Liar was one of them, Mr Cruelty another, and a third was called Mr No-good. They sat down at a long table and began to debate Faithful's case.

The discussion did not last long for every one of them had already made up his mind that the prisoner must die.

"Such a fellow should be put to death without a moment's hesitation," said Mr No-good.

Mr Liar agreed that the man was a villain, and should be killed with all speed.

"Hanging is too good for him," said Mr Cruelty, a pale thin-lipped man. "Let us invent some more painful death."

Minutes after leaving the courtroom, the jurors were

back. Their leader told the Judge that they were agreed without exception that Faithful was guilty.

"Let the prisoner be returned to prison," said the Judge, "and there let him be put to death with all possible cruelty."

When he heard the sentence, Faithful did not flinch. The guards dragged him out of the courtroom and led him away to die. He was whipped and beaten; his flesh was cut with sharp knives. Men threw great stones at his body until he was bruised and bleeding. Last of all, they burned him to ashes at the stake.

Throughout his long ordeal, Faithful showed no sign of pain. His mind was fixed on the everlasting crown of which Evangelist had spoken, and which he knew would soon be his. The townspeople came out to watch his execution, but he paid them no heed. And at the moment of his death his faith was rewarded, for a great miracle took place.

Behind the crowd stood a pair of white horses, beautiful animals who drew a chariot of burnished gold. When Faithful's heart stopped beating, the silver sound of trumpets rang out and his soul was borne to the Heavenly City in the golden chariot. The white horses flew through the air and the spirit of Faithful reached its goal. From now on, he would dwell for ever in Zion with the Lord and all his true servants.

When Christian saw this marvellous sight, he was overcome with joy. He had no fear of his own death, for he knew that he too had been a loyal follower of God.

But for Christian, the journey was not yet finished. His trial was postponed, and he was kept for some time in prison. The guards watched him closely and it seemed beyond his power to escape. But the Lord, who rules all things, did not wish Christian's enemies to have the

satisfaction of putting him to death. One afternoon he caused the guards to fall asleep in the sun. The keys of the jail hung on a chain from the belt of the chief jailer and Christian saw his chance of freedom.

Stealthily he slipped the keys from the ring on which they were carried. He walked to the gate and opened the massive padlock which secured it. The hinges creaked as the gate swung open. But the guards snored on and within an hour the pilgrim was on the outskirts of the town rejoicing over his miraculous escape.

He did not walk alone. A man named Hopeful had joined him as a companion. As they journeyed on together, they talked about the town of Vanity and the torments Christian and his dead friend had endured there.

"Your sufferings were not in vain," said Hopeful. "When I saw your steadfast courage, my heart was moved and I decided to join you in your pilgrimage if ever you escaped.

"I was not the only one. Many other citizens were moved as I was. You may be sure that they will follow my example and become pilgrims like yourself."

Christian was happy to think that although one man had died, another had arisen to take his place. His heart uplifted, he went on his way with his new companion.

14

The Silver Snare

Soon after they had left Vanity behind them, Christian and his new fellow pilgrim caught sight of a traveller some way ahead. They made haste to catch up with him, greeting him and asking where he was from and how far he was planning to journey along the road.

"I am from the town of Fair-speech," answered the stranger, "and I am bound for the Heavenly City."

This man was called By-ends; but he did not reveal his name.

"Fair-speech is said to be a wealthy town," said Christian. "Do you have rich relatives dwelling there?"

"Indeed I do," replied By-ends proudly. "Lord Turnabout, Mr Facing-both-ways, Mr Smooth-man—they're all kindred of mine, and so is the parson of our parish, who goes by the name of Mr Two-tongues."

"And what do you do for a living?" asked Hopeful.

"As for that, you should know that I'm a gentleman of leisure," said By-ends. "However, my great-grandfather was a waterman, who faced one way and rowed the other. You could say that my money came to me in much the same way."

"And are you a married man?"

"I am. My wife is a good woman, a virtuous lady. She's the daughter of Lady Feigning, you know. We're ordinary folk, though—less strict than some in matters of religion, it's true. We differ in two small points. First, if things are against us, well, we never put up a fight. 'Never struggle against wind and tide,' as my great-grandfather always said. Secondly, we prefer our religion to make a fine show. Religion in silver shoes, out in the streets in the sunshine—that's what we like to see."

Christian stopped and drew Hopeful aside.

"I think I know who this is," he whispered. "Unless I'm much mistaken, it's By-ends of Fair-speech. If it is, we are walking with one of the worst knaves in all this country."

"Why don't you ask his name again?" suggested Hopeful. "He can hardly be ashamed to say who he is, surely!"

"Friend," said Christian to By-ends, "I've been listening to your talk, and it has struck me that you know a thing or two more than the average man. Can I be right in thinking that you are By-ends of Fair-speech?"

"That's not my name, though it's what my enemies call me."

"I suppose you must have given them some reason for finding such a nickname for you?"

"Not a bit of it!" protested By-ends. "People envy me because I always happen to make my opinion agree with whatever's fashionable. I can't help that, and if I'm abused for it, I must bear my cross as others have. Let me go with you and you will find that I am pleasant company."

"If you go with us, By-ends, you will face danger and difficulty. You will be going against wind and tide, which you say you never do. You will have to learn how to recognize religion in rags as well as in silver shoes. You will have to keep faith when Faith is bound in iron chains and when he walks the streets amid cheering crowds."

"It's none of your business what I do or believe," was By-ends' sullen reply.

"Not a step further," insisted Christian, "unless you do as we do in these matters."

"In that case," muttered By-ends, "I'll leave you to go on without me. I expect that some more travellers will come along soon and then perhaps I'll meet with someone who appreciates my company."

Christian and Hopeful went on their way. Before long, they saw that By-ends had indeed fallen in with new companions. They were called Mr Hold-the-world, Mr Money-love and Mr Save-all, greedy men whose chief care was to increase their wealth. The four held a long conference, in which By-ends persuaded his fellow travellers to help him in his argument with Christian and Hopeful.

"I think you should speak to them, Hold-the-world," he said. "They've already lost their tempers with me once. Perhaps a fresh voice might move them to throw their lot in with ours."

Hold-the-world, Money-love, Save-all and By-ends quickened their pace until they drew level with the two pilgrims.

"Listen to me," began Hold-the-world. He was sure he was going to outwit Christian and he almost stuttered in his haste to begin the argument. "My friends and I have been having a bit of a chat, and we thought you might like to help us out by answering a couple of questions."

As he said this, Hold-the-world winked foolishly at his cronies.

"Certainly," agreed Christian. "What is it you wish to know?"

"It's like this," explained Hold-the-world. "Suppose you're a man of business—or a parson, too, for the matter of that. You see a chance to get on in the world, improve your position, make a bit more money. Now, to take this chance, you have to give ground on a few small points. There's some question of religious belief that stands in your way. You know, the kind of thing people call a 'matter of principle'."

Hold-the-world sneered as he said this, showing yellow teeth between his plump lips.

"Anyway," he continued, "this is the problem. Should you stick to these fine principles of yours, or is it all right to wink an eye at a point of detail for the sake of getting your hands on a nice heap of gold?"

"We've been talking it over," added By-ends. "We decided that the Lord would hardly mind you altering a point of religion here and there to help you along in the world. Why, a man might take up religion for the sake of gaining new customers for his shop. That must be a good thing for the Lord surely wants us to become religious whatever our reasons."

"Questions such as these are easily answered," said Christian. "We know from the Gospel of St John that it is wrong to follow Christ for the sake of worldly goods. How much worse to make use of the faith as a cover for our own greedy ambition! You may well find others of your opinion, Hold-the-world, but I tell you that they will be nothing but heathens, hypocrites, devils, and witches if they *do* agree with you. This was the religion of the Pharisees; long prayers were their pretence, but to get widows' houses was their intent."

When Christian had finished speaking, he stood waiting for By-ends and his companions to reply. But they said nothing. They shuffled from foot to foot and exchanged sheepish glances, but not one of them opened his mouth to answer the pilgrim's attack.

"Hopeful," said Christian. "Look at these wretches. If the words of a mere man can reduce them to such a pitiful silence, how will they fare when the Almighty comes to judge them with the judgement of roaring flames?"

So saying, he strode off down the path with his friend, leaving Hold-the-world, Money-love, Save-all and By-ends far behind.

After this fierce argument, they were pleased to find themselves crossing the Plain of Ease, a stretch of well-tended and fertile country. Their lungs drank the soft air of the place, and their tired feet sank blissfully into its turf. However, this belt of delicate land did not last long and Christian and Hopeful were soon through it.

The way now led past a small hill, which was known as the Hill of Lucre. A silver-mine had been dug in its side. In former times, many travellers had left the road at this point to see the rare and precious metal. But the ground was deceitful around the entrance to the mine: the solid-seeming earth would give way without warning, and the unwary pilgrim would be pitched into the depths, there to lie for ever, dead or maimed.

As Christian and Hopeful drew close to the mine, they were hailed by a gentlemanly-looking person who introduced himself as Demas and begged them to turn aside and examine the wonders of the hill.

"I can think of nothing which would make me leave the straight and narrow way," said Christian.

"Here is a silver-mine," said Demas. "All may come and dig. The work is light and the reward is large."

"Let's pay a visit to this place," said Hopeful.

Christian's answer was firm. "I shall not leave the path.

I have heard of this place; many have been killed here by the treachery of the ground. What is more, treasure is a hindrance to a pilgrim, and he journeys more easily without it. Demas knows these things as well as I."

Christian fixed his eyes on Demas's face. "Come, friend, will you deny that the place is dangerous?"

"Not very dangerous," replied Demas. But he blushed as he spoke and his voice faltered. It was clear that he was lying.

"Let us go on our way, Hopeful," said Christian.

As they moved on, Hopeful asked his friend what he thought By-ends would do if Demas invited him to explore the mine.

"Oh, he will go, no doubt, and all his companions with him, for that is the kind of people they are. They will all die there, you may be sure."

Demas still called out to them, saying that he was a pilgrim like them, and no enemy. "Come and look!" he cried. "Where's the harm in looking?"

Christian's patience came to an end, and he stopped and turned.

"I know who you are, Demas. Gehazi was your great-grandfather, Judas was your father, and you follow in their wicked footsteps. Judas was hanged for his evil-doing, and you deserve no better fate. You may be certain that when we come to the Eternal City we will give word to the Lord of the cunning trickery you practise here at the Hill of Lucre."

As Christian spoke these angry words, By-ends and his companions came into view. Demas did not reply to the accusations, but turned his attention to the newcomers.

Christian and Hopeful saw the scene clearly enough, though they could not hear what was spoken. Demas beckoned the four travellers to him, nodding and smiling as if he were offering them the finest present in the world. At once they went over to him, breaking into a run in their haste to see the glinting silver. He led them away up the hill. Hopeful and Christian stood a long while waiting for them to return. Demas came back, but of By-ends, Save-all, Money-love and Hold-the-world there was no sign.

Christian turned to his fellow pilgrim and sighed.

"Perhaps they have tumbled over the brink of the pit and fallen to destruction," he said. "Perhaps choking vapours rose to smother them, as often happens in a mine. Perhaps they are sweating and grunting in the bowels of the hill, imprisoned in the dark.

"At any rate, one thing is certain. They will never again be seen on the way which leads to the Heavenly City."

15

Doubting Castle

Not far beyond the Hill of Lucre, the pilgrims came upon a curious monument. It was a pillar, shaped like a woman and made of salt. At first they could not make sense of it. Then Hopeful noticed an inscription above the head of the figure.

"This is some foreign tongue," he said, "and I am no scholar. Christian, can you unriddle this message?"

Christian stood looking at the strange letters until he had worked out their meaning.

"It says: REMEMBER LOT'S WIFE," he told his friend. "She was a citizen of the wicked city of Sodom. The Lord gave her the chance of safety, but she stopped in her flight when the city was being destroyed, and looked back longingly at her old home. As a punishment for hesitation, she was transformed into this pillar of salt that we see here."

Hopeful stood silent, gazing at the marvellous sight.

"My brother," said Christian seriously, "there is a lesson for us in this. If we had accepted Demas's invitation to look at the silver-mines of Lucre, then we, like this woman, might have made ourselves a spectacle for those who followed."

"And it was I who wanted to leave the way and go with him!" exclaimed Hopeful bitterly. "Lot's wife only looked back; but I wanted to follow temptation with my feet as well as my eyes. I am ashamed that I ever felt such wicked desire. We must give thanks that we have been spared the fate of this wretched woman and we must keep her in our minds as we continue our journey."

The way led across a plain to a pleasant river, called by King David the River of God, and by John the Baptist the River of the Water of Life. The pilgrims were delighted to find that their path lay along its banks. Flourishing trees grew all around them, laden with fruit. The travellers refreshed themselves by drinking deeply of the crystal-clear water and eating the fruit. The leaves of the trees, too, were good for medicine, and by chewing them Christian and Hopeful protected themselves from the fevers which so often attack wayfarers.

On either side of the river lay broad meadows, the thick green grass full of white lilies. All the year round these water-meadows were fertile for the river never ran dry.

"Let us rest in this beautiful country," said Christian. "There will be trials enough for us before we reach our goal. As we are in a place of safety for once, we should take this opportunity of refreshing ourselves for the struggles which lie ahead."

So the two travellers lay down at dusk in the soft grass and slept peacefully until morning. When they awoke, they again gathered fruit from the overhanging trees, and again drank deeply of the clear water. Fatigue left their limbs; strength returned to them. For several days they stayed on the banks of the life-giving stream. But they had not yet come to their journey's end. One morning they decided that it was time to set off once more for the Heavenly City.

They had not gone far before the path left the river-bank. This was a disappointment for them both. The track became rough and steep and their feet began to ache.

"We dare not leave the way," said Christian, "but I wish it were a bit easier!"

Hopeful said nothing, but his face showed that he, too, was tired and discouraged.

When they had walked for some time in this dejected humour, they came to a stile on the left of the road. Beyond this lay By-path Meadow where the grass grew thick and soft.

Christian climbed the stile and looked into the field.

"There's a path running along the other side of the fence," he called. "It follows the road, and it'll be much easier for our feet. Come on, Hopeful, let's take it."

"But what if it should lead us out of our way?"

"That's not likely," said Christian.

Hopeful was persuaded, and the pilgrims climbed over into the meadow. It was indeed easier for their feet, and they strode along happily until they saw another traveller ahead of them. This man was called Vain-confidence. Christian called out to him and he waited for them to catch him up.

"Where does this track lead, friend?" asked Hopeful.

"To the gates of the Celestial City," he replied.

"You see? What did I tell you!" said Christian triumphantly.

Vain-confidence led the way and the pilgrims followed. All seemed well until suddenly the light began to fail. They could hardly believe that day was over already; but it grew darker and darker, and soon Vain-confidence could no longer be seen.

"I wonder how our new friend is faring," said Christian anxiously.

At that moment a horrible shout rang out ahead of

them. Vain-confidence, unable to see where he was going, had fallen into a pit dug by the Devil. This was a trap for unwary travellers. He fell to the bottom, and was dashed to pieces. When Christian called out to him, asking what had happened, there was no answer but a moan of agony.

"Where are we now?" asked Hopeful.

Christian was silent. It was his fault; he had chosen to take this path and now they were lost. They stood in the darkness, at the edge of the pit, in despair. Thunder growled in the sky and heavy drops of rain fell ominously around them.

"If only we had kept to the right way!" groaned Hopeful.

"But who would have thought we would get lost so easily?"

"I was afraid of it all along, but as you are older than me I took your advice," said Hopeful.

As he spoke, a flash of lightning split the clouds. The storm was breaking. The rain began to fall with terrible violence. Streams of water rushed about their feet. Soon the path was a foaming torrent which threatened to sweep the pilgrims away and dash them on the black rocks which rose all about them.

"My brother," said Christian wretchedly, "do not be angry with me. Even though I have brought you into danger, I never wished to do it."

"Take comfort," replied Hopeful. "I willingly forgive you. Perhaps this trial will be for our good."

Then Christian said he would walk in front so that he would be the first to meet the dangers of the way. Hopeful protested.

"Your mind is troubled, Christian, and you may lose the path in your unhappiness. Let me go first, my friend."

Then a miracle took place which filled their hearts with fresh hope. Above the hideous roaring of the storm a clear voice spoke to them.

"Let your heart think of the high way," said the voice. *"Turn again, and seek the road that you were following before."*

The way back was far from easy. The water had risen to their knees, and with every step they risked losing their foothold and being dashed to the ground. It was so dark that they could not see a foot in front of them.

"We will never reach the stile tonight," shouted Christian. "Do you see those bushes at the side of the road?"

Hopeful strained his eyes. He glimpsed, through the the darkness and falling rain, a clump of bushes growing on a bank just above them. There at least they would be safe from the flood and the branches might give them some shelter from the downpour.

"Let's creep in under there, Hopeful, and try to get some rest before dawn. When it gets light we can fight our way back to the high road."

The exhausted pilgrims struggled up the bank and dragged themselves in beneath the bushes. Gradually the storm's fury grew less and the rain stopped falling. Christian and Hopeful lay sleeping, both praying that when day broke they would be safe.

They did not know where they were. Not far from the place where they lay was a grim old fortress, Doubting Castle by name. This was the home of Giant Despair, a savage tyrant who had put scores of travellers to death. It was in the Giant's grounds that the pilgrims had fallen asleep. He rose early the next morning and found them lying in his fields. Tired out by their struggle with the storm, they slept peacefully. But the Giant had no pity for them.

"Wake up!" he shouted in a grim and surly voice. "Wake up, you wretches, and tell me what you are doing trespassing on my lands!"

16

Giant Despair

When Christian and Hopeful opened their eyes, the first thing they saw was the terrible figure of Despair looming above them.

"Where do you come from? What are you doing in the grounds of Doubting Castle?" he asked them in his grisly voice.

They tried to answer him, but before they had finished explaining that they were pilgrims who had lost their way, he broke in saying,

"During the night you trampled on my fields and when you lay down beneath this bush you were trespassing. You must come with me into the castle!"

Christian and Hopeful had no strength to resist such a brute. He was twice as tall as they, and his brawny arms were thick and knotted like the roots of an oak. He drove them down the path to his castle. When they arrived, he threw them into a stinking dungeon where the light of the sun was never seen. The foul air of the place depressed their spirits. Lack of food soon made matters worse, for they were to be locked in this place for four long days without a drop to drink or a scrap to eat.

"My suffering is worse than yours, Hopeful," said Christian to his friend, "for it is all through me that we are here. If I had listened to you, we would never have strayed from the straight and narrow path."

Hopeful tried to encourage him, but it was hardly possible to kindle a spark of cheerfulness while they lay prisoners in the castle dungeon.

Despair had a wife as grim as himself, a hag whose name was Diffidence. No hopeful thought had ever entered her soul, and she was bent on making others as miserable as herself.

"My dear," said Despair to Diffidence, "I have some new prisoners in our dungeon. I caught them trespassing on our land. What shall I do with them?"

"When you get up in the morning, beat them without pity!" she said, her red eyes glinting with hatred.

Next morning the pilgrims were woken from their uneasy sleep by the giant's echoing footsteps. He flung open the door of their cell and strode across the stone floor to them, grasping a heavy club. With this club, made of the wood of the sour-fruited crab-tree, he began to belabour them until their bodies were covered with weals and bruises. They lay groaning on the floor, unable to move for their injuries. When he had finished with them, Despair turned and left them to their misery, locking the door behind him.

All that day they saw neither food nor drink. The time passed miserably; they tried to sympathize with one another in their distress, but pain and anguish crushed their hearts.

"Well?" asked Diffidence that evening. "Did you give them a thorough beating, as you said you would?"

"I did," answered Despair.

"And did you make an end of their wretched lives?"

"They were still breathing when I left them."

"This is my advice," hissed Diffidence. "Go to them tomorrow and persuade them to kill themselves. It'll be the easiest way out in the long run."

When morning came, Giant Despair went down into the gloomy depths of Doubting Castle and opened the door of the pilgrims' cell.

"Do you see this, you miserable rogues?" he asked. "Here are sharp knives. By cutting your throats you will put yourselves out of your misery. There's a dish of poison, too; one sip of that and it'll all be over for you both."

Christian and Hopeful stared up at him in fear and horror.

"Or take hold of this halter, hitch it round a beam, and you can break your own necks. Why should you choose life, since for you it is so full of bitterness?"

The pilgrims looked at one another.

"I speak for us both," said Christian firmly, "when I say that we have only one desire, and that is that you should give us our freedom. While there is a hope of reaching the Heavenly City, we will never be so cowardly as to take our own lives."

At this, Despair let out a savage roar. Raising his arm above his head, he lunged across the room at them. But at that moment, far above in the world outside, the morning sun broke through the mist. In sunny weather, Despair often fell victim to fits, and when the fit was on him, the strength left his limbs and he became as feeble as a chicken. As the sun touched the field before the castle, his hand fell weakly to his side. He turned and stumbled to the door.

Alone once more, Christian and Hopeful debated the giant's advice.

"What shall we do, my brother?" said Christian. "This life of ours is nothing but misery and I would sooner be strangled than suffer these tortures any longer."

"Take courage!" answered Hopeful. "It is a great sin to

commit murder. But the man who kills another kills only his body, while the man who kills himself destroys both body and soul. Besides, Giant Despair is not the ruler of the world, and the Lord may have plans to free us. The tyrant may die; he may forget to lock us in; he may be seized by another of his fits. While he is powerless, perhaps we will escape from this dreadful place.''

The long day passed. All was black in the dungeon; nothing marked the slow movement of the sun. Towards evening, the corridor shook once more with the giant's stride, and his grisly visage appeared at the door.

"What!" he cried furiously. "You have not followed my advice? Wretched men, it will be the worse for you! I am going to my wife. I'm sure she will tell me the shortest way to deal with you.''

As his footsteps died away, Christian fell into a swoon, overcome with terror.

"Why be downhearted? Think of the dangers you have already faced,'' said Hopeful. "You did battle with Apollyon, the fiend with the face of the lion, and the Lord gave you victory. You walked unharmed through the Valley of the Shadow of Death. When you were trapped in the cage at Vanity Fair, your body hung with chains, you never lost your determination. Will you let this giant be the death of you after all the triumphs you have known? Shame on you, Christian!''

In her gloomy bedchamber, Diffidence was haranguing her husband and egging him on to put an end to his prisoners.

"They didn't take your advice? They refused to kill themselves?'' she screamed. "I know what I would do if I were you. I'd drag them out into the castle yard and show them the pile of bones and skulls. You can say, 'Look! This is all that's left of my former prisoners. I tore every one of them in pieces with my bare hands. Before the week is out, I plan to do the same with you.'"

Next morning Christian and Hopeful were overjoyed to be led out into the open air. But the high walls of the courtyard shut out the sun and all they saw was a pile of skeletons heaped up to the height of a man.

"Other pilgrims have trespassed here before," said Despair brutally. "I tore them limb from limb. You see for yourselves what is left of them. Your bones, too, will be piled here within the week."

So saying, he flourished his crab-tree cudgel and beat the pilgrims back to their subterranean cell.

"They're still alive," said Despair that night. "They must be hoping that they'll find some way out. Otherwise they would have killed themselves long ago."

"In the morning, search them for keys," said Diffidence. "If they've been plotting to escape, punish them with a worse beating than any you've yet given them. That ought to finish them off!"

It was sound advice that the hag gave her husband, but it came too late. During that night, Christian gave a sudden cry of joy and amazement.

"Hopeful! Do you see what I have here?"

He showed his companion a key of shining silver which hung on a chain around his neck.

"What is it?" asked Hopeful.

"Fool that I am, to have lain so long in this stinking dungeon!" replied Christian. "This is the key called Promise, and I know for sure that it will open any lock in Doubting Castle. It has been hanging over my heart all this time and only now have I remembered it."

"Let's waste no time, my brother," said Hopeful. "It must be near day, and our jailer will soon be coming down to us."

The door of their cell opened easily when the key was fitted into the lock. The two pilgrims, sore from their wounds but eager for freedom, climbed the slimy steps which led up to the courtyard. The door into the yard was opened, too, though less easily than the door of the cell.

The massive outer gate was an even more difficult obstacle. The key called Promise fitted the keyhole, but at first it seemed that the lock was so stiff with rust that it was beyond the pilgrims' power to force it open. Their plight grew more desperate with every moment. The sun was climbing the sky; it could not be long before Despair awoke.

At last the gate swung open. Its huge hinges groaned and shrieked and the noise woke the giant. He sprang to the window. When he saw the pilgrims escaping, rage overwhelmed him. He reached for his terrible club, determined that this time he would beat them to death.

But as his hand stretched out for the weapon, the fit seized him. The sun shone full in his eyes and his arm fell limply to his side. He was powerless; he watched in a frenzy as the prisoners hurried to safety, but there was nothing he could do to stop them.

As soon as they were out of the grounds of Doubting Castle, Christian and Hopeful made haste to return to the straight and narrow way.

"We are safe!" cried Christian, as they stood once more in the road. "This is the King's Highway, and Despair has no power to touch us while we walk in it."

"Here is the stile we climbed over," said Hopeful. "Surely we should leave some warning, so that other pilgrims do not make our mistake and fall into the cruel hands of Giant Despair?"

So they built a pillar of stones, and wrote upon it a

message for all those who followed in their footsteps: OVER THIS STILE IS THE WAY TO DOUBTING CASTLE, WHICH IS KEPT BY GIANT DESPAIR, AN ENEMY OF THE LORD WHO SEEKS TO DESTROY HIS HOLY PILGRIMS.

Thanks to this message, many travellers were saved from a terrible fate. Despair and Diffidence now dwell alone in the gloom of Doubting Castle. From one year's end to the next they have hardly a victim for their hideous cruelty.

17

The Delectable Mountains

Christian and Hopeful went on their way until they arrived in a fertile region of gardens, vineyards, and orchards. Fountains of living water sprang up around them. They washed the dust of the road from their weary limbs, drank deeply, and ate the juicy, purple grapes which grew on the terraced hill sides.

"I know this country," said Christian. "It seems a long while since I first saw it. That was when I stayed in the Palace Beautiful as the guest of Prudence, Piety and Charity. One clear dawn I saw this beautiful land in the distance and was told that it was called the country of the Delectable Mountains."

The way led up through the orchards and on to a high plateau where flocks of sheep nibbled the tender grass. The pilgrims went up to one of the shepherds tending these flocks and asked him who was the lord of these pastures.

"These mountains are Emmanuel's Land, the pastures of the Lord," replied the shepherd. "We are within sight of his Heavenly City. These sheep too are his; indeed, he gave his life to save them from death."

"So this must be the way to the Heavenly City!" cried Christian eagerly. "How much further do we have to go?"

"The distance is too great for all but those who shall surely get there."

"And is the journey safe, or is it full of peril?"

"It is safe for those who are to be saved, but the wicked perish at the side of the road."

"Is there any resting-place for pilgrims weary of travelling?" asked Christian.

"The Lord has charged us to entertain strangers. All the good things of the country are yours to enjoy," replied the shepherd. "Come with me to our camp, where you will be able to eat and sleep."

The tents were pitched in the shade of a silver-leaved olive grove. While Christian and Hopeful ate and drank, their hosts—whose names were Knowledge, Experience, Watchful, and Sincere—asked them about their journey.

"How have you succeeded in coming so far?" Sincere wanted to know. "Many set out on the path which you have travelled, but few reach the slopes of the Delectable Mountains."

As the travellers unfolded the history of their adventures, the shepherds looked lovingly on them, knowing that they were true pilgrims.

"Stay with us tonight," said Experience, "and in the morning we will show you the wonders of the place."

Christian and Hopeful were happy to accept. That night they slept sweetly beneath the stars, breathing the pure and delicate mountain air. They awoke filled with strength and walked with their hosts over the springy turf until they reached the top of a steep hill where the ground fell away before them in a sheer drop.

"This is the Hill of Error," said Watchful. "Look down the precipice and tell me what you see."

Hopeful did as he was told. In a trembling voice he said, "I see the bodies of travellers, dashed to pieces where they have fallen from the brink of this cliff."

"Many have been the victims of error," said Watchful.

"They have held false beliefs and in their blindness have stumbled to destruction. Their bodies lie as you see them, unburied, as a warning to those who come after."

Christian and Hopeful fell into a thoughtful silence. They followed their guides to the summit of another hill from which they saw a sight which chilled their blood. Experience pointed into the distance, and they beheld a dreary churchyard, full of massive tombstones. Among these stumbled a band of men. From their movements it was clear that they were blind: their trembling fingers were stretched out piteously before them, but they still found themselves tripping over the stones and falling headlong to the ground.

"This hill is called Caution," explained Experience. "These men are the victims of Giant Despair. Do you see where a path leaves the highway on the left, crossing a stile into By-path Meadow? That path leads to Doubting Castle, Despair's fortress. These men all turned aside from the highway and fell prisoner to him. When he had kept them awhile in the dungeons of Doubting Castle, he put out their eyes and led them among these tombs where he left them to wander to this very day. The saying of the wise man is fulfilled: *he that wanders out of the way of understanding shall remain in the congregation of the dead.*"

As they listened, Christian and Hopeful felt their eyes fill with tears. Ashamed of their past folly, they said nothing to the good shepherds, but looked at one another in secret gladness that they had been saved from the fate of the blind wanderers among the tombstones.

"One sight remains for you to see," said Sincere. "This is not a mountain-top, but a gloomy valley, for it is one of the entrances to Hell. To find it we must climb down into the sunless depths."

They came at length to a craggy bottom, filled with the stench of brimstone. Sincere and the other shepherds rolled aside a boulder and told the pilgrims to look into the bowels of the hill. Flames cast a lurid glow on the sides of the cavern, and the air was loud with the cries of the damned.

"It is through this by-way that hypocrites make their way to Hell," said Sincere. "Esau, who sold his birthright, went this way; and so did Judas, who sold his loving master. These men began as pilgrims, but they left the straight and narrow way."

Christian and Hopeful looked at one another. "We shall have to seek strength from the Lord," they said, "if we are to reach our journey's end."

"Yes," said the shepherds, "and if you find strength, you will have need of it. Others have got further than these mountains, and still fallen by the way."

The pilgrims felt that the time had come for them to continue on their journey. Their hearts were heavy and their limbs trembled at the warnings they had been shown and they longed to bring their pilgrimage to a safe end.

"Before you leave us," said Knowledge, "let us show you a sight to give you firmer hope. If you climb with us to the top of the hill called Clear, and look through our glass, you will see before you the shining gates of Zion."

Although their hands shook at the memory of the terrors they had witnessed, the pilgrims held the glass steady enough to see in the distance the longed-for walls of the Heavenly City, and to make out something of its glory.

"This sight, dim as it is, will give us the strength we need," said Christian. "And now, my friends, we must leave you, thanking you from our hearts for the kindness you have shown us."

With these words, he took his staff and set off along the highway with Hopeful at his side. Sincere warned the pilgrims of two dangers which lay before them: the danger of Flatterer, and the danger of sleeping in the Enchanted Ground.

"If you can escape these two traps," said Sincere, "you will arrive at the shores of the perilous river. Once there, Zion lies before you on the further bank. Farewell, my friends, and may good fortune be yours."

A little beyond the Delectable Mountains, to the left of the path, lies the country of Conceit, and from this land a narrow lane joins the highway. As the pilgrims passed the entrance to this crooked lane, a brisk young lad came out onto the highway and began to walk along with them.

"I'm from Conceit," said the lad, whose name was Ignorance, "and I'm on my way to the Heavenly City. Are you going there too?"

"When you arrive at the gate, I think you may find some difficulty in entering," said Christian. "Have you anything to show there? I was given a scroll, which I have with me now. Have you received any such token?"

"Don't worry about me," replied Ignorance cheerfully. "I've not led a bad life on the whole, and I think I've got a fair idea of what the Lord expects. I've always said my prayers, given money to the poor, and that kind of thing."

"At the beginning of the journey, I had to go through a little gate," said Christian. "But you just walked down that crooked lane. I fear that you will be taken for a thief who climbed in by the back way."

"As for that little gate," said Ignorance, "everyone knows that it's miles from here. We're lucky, you see, in my country. We just stroll down the lane and there we are, right in the highway to Zion. I don't suppose anyone could have told me the way to your precious gate, even if I'd bothered to ask. In Conceit, we're happy to take the short cut, my friend. You stick to your ways and we'll stick to ours."

Christian realized that this lad was wise in his own eyes, however great a fool he might appear to others.

"Hopeful," he whispered, "there is no point in talking to him just now. Perhaps he will come to realize his own folly and then he may have ears for what we have to tell him. But for the moment, let us walk on ahead of him."

"I agree with you," said Hopeful. "It's a mistake to try and explain too much to him, the more so while he is in his present humour. We will go on ahead. Later, perhaps, we can wait for him to catch us up."

So the two pilgrims went on ahead, and Ignorance walked behind.

18

The Web of Flattery

Soon after they had overtaken Ignorance, the pilgrims found themselves in a narrow and gloomy stretch of the road. The place seemed evil: they were not surprised when a scene of great misery met their eyes. They saw a poor wretch, bound by seven strong cords, being carried off by seven lusty devils, who were dragging him back to the cave in the craggy valley, where they would force him down the road to Hell.

"Who was that?" asked Hopeful.

It had been hard to recognize the prisoner, for he had hung his head in shame, like one caught in the act of stealing.

"I thought it might be my old acquaintance Turnaway, a citizen of Apostasy, the town of broken vows. However, I am not sure. Such robberies and kidnappings as this happen every day in this dark passage, which is called Dead Man's Lane because of all the murders which are committed here."

"If thieves set upon me," said Hopeful, "I would give them a hard time!"

"Until it has happened, you can never be sure," replied Christian. "Let me tell you the story of Little-faith, who was set upon in this very place. Three sturdy rogues, brothers named Guilt, Faint-heart and Mistrust, galloped up to him here and told him to stand and deliver. They made short work of him when he tried to resist: Guilt knocked him over the head with a heavy club, and he was left for dead by the side of the road. When he came to, he found all his money gone. All he had left were his scroll and his jewels."

"His jewels!" cried Hopeful. "Surely he could have exchanged them for cash?"

"You don't understand," replied Christian. "Without the jewels, he could never have entered the Holy City. Besides, they were of no value in this world. Little-faith, although weak, was a good man, and he never thought of pawning or exchanging them."

"Why, then, is he known as Little-faith?"

"Because he could not stop grieving for the loss of his money, I suppose. I tell you this story, Hopeful, to show how easy it is to be robbed whn you are on the highway. This man could hardly bear to be parted from his gold and silver, yet the three brothers found it easy enough to steal every penny he had. They might have made an end of him, too, had they not heard someone coming, and run away for fear that it might be Great-grace, the Lord's champion."

"Who is this Great-grace?"

"He is the defender of the Lord's servants," replied Christian. "You may think you can look after yourself, but unless you are one in a thousand, you need help and protection, just as Little-faith did. Every pilgrim should ask for two things: a shield to defend himself with and a companion for the journey. The Lord himself will be with us, if only we ask for his help. Do not boast that you could defend yourself, my friend. With the Lord, we will defeat every robber we meet; without him, we may fall victim to the first who crosses our path."

When Christian had finished telling the story of Little-faith, the pilgrims found themselves at a fork in the way. It was difficult to know whether they should take the left-hand or the right-hand path, for each seemed as straight as the other. So they stood for some time in doubt until a stranger came up to them, a man whose skin was dark although he was dressed in light-coloured clothes.

"Why are you standing here, my friends?" he asked.

"We are going to the Celestial City," replied Hopeful, "but we do not know which is the right way."

"I, too, am going there," said the stranger. "Come with me. It's an easy journey from here."

They followed him along the left-hand path, and were soon aware that the road was gradually turning away from the direction which they had been taking, until both felt sure that their backs were to Zion, and that every step they took was leading them away from their goal.

"I am uneasy," said Christian to his companion. "Do you think this is truly the right way?"

Before Hopeful could answer, the pilgrims felt themselves trapped in a fine net. Their limbs were powerless; they were caught like flies in the deadly mesh of a spider's web. Terrified, they turned their eyes on their guide. As they watched, the clothes fell from him and they saw him in all his black wickedness, gloating over the disaster which had befallen them.

"We should have listened more carefully to the warnings of the shepherds!" cried Hopeful. "They told us of a man named Flatterer, yet we took a stranger's advice when we were lost. He has undone us. We will never reach our journey's end, never cross the river and stand at the gates of the Heavenly City."

The pilgrims lay paralysed in the cruel web, weeping tears of remorse and despair until at last they saw in the distance a Shining One coming to their rescue, an angel with a stern face and in his hand a whipcord.

"Who are you?" asked the Shining One. "How do you come to be prisoners in this deadly net?"

Christian answered that they were poor pilgrims on their way to Zion who had taken the word of a dark man dressed in light clothing. "He told us to follow him, saying that he too was going to the Heavenly City."

"That man was Flatterer, a false apostle in the disguise of an angel of light," explained the Shining One. "Tell me, did you not stay last night in the Delectable Mountains?"

"We did," replied Hopeful.

"And did the shepherds not warn you of the dangers of the way and tell you to beware of Flatterer?"

The pilgrims had to admit that the shepherds had indeed given them warning.

"I shall set you free," said the Shining One. "But before you can continue your journey, I shall have to punish you for your folly. Those whom I love, I also punish."

And he made the pilgrims lie on the ground while he whipped them with the cord.

"And now," he said gently, "go on your way, and take more care whom you trust, my friends."

Christian and Hopeful thanked the Shining One for setting them free. Once more they had been rescued from peril, and could hope to finish their pilgrimage at the gates of Zion. Singing joyfully, they went on their way.

After a while, they saw a man coming down the road with his back towards the Celestial City. When he was face to face with the pilgrims, the newcomer asked them scornfully where they were going.

"To Mount Zion," they replied.

At this, the man burst out laughing. He laughed until he cried, as if he had just heard the best joke of his life. His name was Atheist, and he had no faith.

"Why are you laughing?" asked Christian.

"To see what fools you are," replied Atheist. "What a tedious journey you have embarked on! What's more, you will get no reward at the end of it, I can assure you."

"What makes you say that? Don't you think we will be welcomed there?"

"Welcomed!" snorted Atheist. "There's no such place, you idiot. It's nothing but a dream! There's no such place in the world."

"No," said Christian. "But there is in the world to come."

"That's what they told me twenty years ago, when I was at home. I, too, have been a fool in my time, you see. I set out full of bright visions to look for this famous City. But I've spent long enough on that search. The time has come for me to abandon the quest. I'm going home as fast as my legs will carry me. When I get there I mean to have a good time, I can tell you, to make up for the years I've wasted walking this stony path."

Christian turned to Hopeful. "Is there any truth, do you think, in what this man says?"

"Beware, for he is one of the flatterers," said Hopeful. "He tells us there is no Mount Zion. In that case, what was it that the shepherds pointed out to us when we stood on top of the hill called Clear? Do not listen to him, I say. Let us go on, or the Shining One with his whip will be upon us again!"

"My brother," said Christian, "I did not ask you because I myself was in doubt, but to show this man a proof of your honest heart. He is blinded by the worship of this world, and cannot see the truth of Heaven. But you have shown him that we have faith. Let us walk on in that faith, knowing that we see the Truth where Atheist sees nothing but what is in front of his nose."

So the two pilgrims went on their way while Atheist, laughing scornfully, walked back down the path, his back still turned towards the Heavenly City.

19
Crossing the Enchanted Ground

The pilgrims were now crossing a dreary plain. The road stretched ahead as straight as a ruler. Nothing broke the monotony of the bare and level expanse.

"I'm beginning to feel drowsy," said Hopeful. "This landscape is making my eyes tired. Let's lie down for a few minutes at the side of the road and have a little rest."

"By no means!" replied Christian sharply. "Once we are asleep, we may never wake again."

"What makes you say that, my brother? Everyone who works needs to sleep. If we take a nap, we will be refreshed for the end of our journey."

"Have you forgotten what Sincere told us in the Delectable Mountains? He warned us to beware of sleeping in the Enchanted Ground. This must be the country he was talking about. Let us not sleep like other men but keep our wits about us and press on with our pilgrimage."

Hopeful confessed that he had made a terrible mistake.

"How glad I am that I am not alone! The wise man was right when he said that two were better than one. Time and again you have saved me. You will have your reward, brother Christian."

They walked on through the barren land, both oppressed with weariness of body and spirit. At each step their eyes fell shut and they had to force themselves to keep going. It was as if they were explorers caught in a blizzard. Sleep was what they longed for, but they knew that to lie down and close their eyes was to abandon all hope of life.

"Come," said Christian when they had trudged another mile. "We must talk to one another. That will keep us awake. There is something I have been meaning to ask you ever since we set out together on the road from Vanity. Tell me, Hopeful, how did you come to join me in my pilgrimage?"

"It's a long story."

"All the better," said Christian. "It will while away the time until we are clear of this dismal country."

"Living as I did in Vanity," began Hopeful, "I was in love with the goods for sale in the Fair. The gorgeous trinkets of the world enchanted me. I shared the customs of the place, too—drinking, lying, swearing, rioting. I was as merry a wretch as anyone in the city.

"Then the time came when my eyes were opened to other things. You and Faithful—Faithful, who was put to death by Hate-good, the most vile of sinners—you two made me see that my life was death, as far as my soul went. I knew that if I carried on in my old ways the anger of the Lord was sure to fall on me in the end."

"And when you realized this, your life was changed?"

"Not at once," replied Hopeful. "For a long time I tried to ignore the danger. From time to time, I would be reminded of it. I would see a dead man carried out of a house or hear the bell tolling for a funeral. Then I would shiver for a moment, as if a draught of cold air had brushed past me. Still, most of the time I went on in the old fashion, as I have said—drinking, brawling, buying gaudy trifles at the Fair."

"Had you any idea how to rid yourself of the weight of sin, when you felt it crushing you?" asked Christian.

"I thought that it was too late. My past wickedness seemed to tell so heavily against me. I felt like a man who runs up a debt with a shopkeeper. He borrows and borrows until he owes a hundred pounds. What good will it do him if one day he decides to start paying on the nail? Unless he can find some way of returning what he has already borrowed, the shopkeeper can haul him up in front of the court and have him flung in jail whenever he wants to.

"I thought it was like that with the Lord. I was in despair whenever I thought of my sins. Then one day Faithful explained to me that the Lord was no shopkeeper and that all the wrong I had ever done could be forgiven me if I was prepared to make the choice."

"What did Faithful tell you to do?" asked Christian.

"He told me that Jesus died for us, and that if I prayed I would be granted sight of him, and would know I was forgiven."

"And you prayed, and you saw him?"

"The first time I saw nothing. It was the same the second time, and the sixth time too. Then one day I was in the blackest despair. Far from thinking of Jesus, I was brooding on my own wickedness. I was thinking of Hell, where I thought I was surely bound.

"It was then that I saw him—not indeed with the eyes of my body, but with the eyes of my understanding. He looked down at me from the pure light of Heaven, saying: *Believe in me, and you will be saved.*

"I told him how great my sins were, and that I was unworthy of his love. I felt like a man covered with dirt, and was ashamed to enter the beautiful palace of Heaven. But I was reminded by the Lord that Jesus died for sinners, and my dirt had been washed away by his blood."

"Tell me," said Christian, "what effect did this vision have on your spirit?"

"From that moment I was filled with the beauty of Jesus. I felt the shamefulness of my old life more strongly than ever and vowed to love nothing but holiness. So it was that I became a pilgrim, and left the deathly comforts of Vanity for the life-giving trials of the straight and narrow way."

When Hopeful had finished his story, the pilgrims walked on in silence for some while. They were still in the dreary land of the Enchanted Ground, though on the horizon the landscape seemed to change, as far as they could judge at such a distance.

"How much further have we to travel in this desert?" asked Hopeful.

"How should I know? But perhaps it is not too far. Besides, I have remembered something. We agreed that we would speak with Ignorance later in our journey and see whether any change had come over him. Perhaps the time has come when he will listen to us."

They looked back and saw Ignorance toiling along the flat track towards them. At long last he drew level, weary, but with a grin on his face.

"How are things with you now?" said Christian by way of greeting. "How does it stand between you and God?"

"All is well, as far as I know."

"And what makes you so sure of that?"

"It's a feeling," said Ignorance. "It's just something I feel in my heart."

Christian turned to Hopeful.

"When will this man realize that we should not judge ourselves by our feelings?"

"Wait a minute," said Ignorance. "That's not the only thing. My life is good, too, as I think I told you last time we met."

"And what makes you believe in the goodness of your life?"

"My—my—." Ignorance seemed confused. "My heart tells me that my life is good."

"We cannot judge by the feelings of the heart. We must look at ourselves in the light of Scripture. Then it will be plain to us that our hearts are wicked and cannot be trusted."

"But what about Jesus?" protested Ignorance. "If I stick to the rules, surely he will help me out?"

"You don't understand a thing!" cried Christian. "It's you that Jesus loves, not what you do. You must give yourself up to him. It's no use asking him for a helping hand, and saying, 'I followed the rules, now do your share!' The only course is to recognize your own wickedness and fly to Jesus as your refuge from the terror of your own sin."

"Wait a minute," said Ignorance. "Are you saying that it doesn't matter what you do, so long as you run to Jesus? In that case, we can all go on in our old ways— drinking and guzzling and living in idleness and luxury."

At this, Christian finally lost his temper. "Ignorance is your name," he said bitterly, "and by nature you are ignorant indeed. If you knew the first thing about the love of Jesus, you would realize that anyone who truly felt that love would at once become incapable of such wickedness as you describe. But it's clear that we are wasting our breath talking to you. Come, Hopeful, I see that you and I must walk without a companion."

The pilgrims quickened their pace, leaving Ignorance behind on the dusty track.

"Such fellows as that are afraid to face their own sinfulness," said Christian. "Rather than realize that they are nothing until God is in their hearts, they trust to their own judgement, and tell themselves that they are leading lives of wisdom and virtue."

"Christian," asked Hopeful, "do you think we are nearing the end of this desolate landscape?"

"Why, are you tired of my conversation?"

"Of course not. I just wondered how much longer we would have to trudge across the Enchanted Ground, not daring to sleep for fear we will never wake, and oppressed all the while by the country's dreariness."

"I am not sure," replied Christian, "but I think the prospect is brightening. Within a mile or two we may find ourselves in a pleasanter place."

Christian's guess was right. Before an hour had passed, the travellers were in the midst of the rich pastures of Beulah, the borderlands of Heaven and the abode of the Shining Ones.

20

The Shining Ones

The land of Beulah surpassed in beauty all the wondrous countries Christian and Hopeful had visited in the course of their pilgrimage. The air there was sweet and pleasant, filled with the sound of birdsong and the scent of flowers. The sun shone by night as well as by day, for this land was beyond the Valley of the Shadow of Death, and Doubting Castle could not be seen. The Heavenly City was in view, and here walked the Shining Ones. The weary pilgrims had all that they wanted. Everything they had longed for during the trials of the journey was to be found in abundance. Fields of wheat shone in the light and grapes hung thickly from rows of flourishing vines. Bread and wine satisfied hunger and thirst and refreshing sleep filled the travellers with new strength. Miraculous voices rang out—welcoming them to Zion and hailing them as the holy people, the chosen ones of the Lord.

Christian and Hopeful followed the path through the heart of this blessed region until they drew near to the Celestial City. The sight almost blinded them in its brilliance. Every street was paved with shining gold. The buildings of pearl and precious stones glittered in the rays of the sun.

At first they were unable to bear so much brightness, and fell sick with longing. They lay on the ground, calling for the Lord and crying out for love of him. But gradually their strength grew and they were able to draw nearer and nearer to the miraculous vision. Their way still ran through orchards and vineyards of unmatched richness, tended by a wise old gardener who led them among the purple grapes and bade them eat.

"Tell me," asked Christian, "whose are all these delicious fruits? Whose is this wonderful garden?"

"This is the garden of the Lord," replied the old man. "He set it out for his own joy, and for the comfort of all pilgrims who arrive here from the world."

When they had eaten their fill of the ripe grapes, Christian and Hopeful fell into a deep sleep. In their slumber they spoke strange things, more than they had ever said while awake. This was no wonder, for the fruit in this garden had magical power, and its sweetness was so great that all who ate it uttered wise words in their sleep.

When they awoke, the pilgrims made their way towards the City of Zion. Because they could not bear its brightness, they gazed at it through a screen of smoked glass which the gardener had given them. As they travelled on, they met with two of the Shining Ones, tall men in costumes of gold.

"Where have you come from? Who have you stayed with, and what dangers did you face on the way?" the strangers asked them.

Christian and Hopeful told them the story of their journey—the dreadful dungeon of Despair, the kind shepherds, the meeting with Ignorance, and the many adventures which had befallen them both before and after their meeting on the outskirts of Vanity.

When their tale was told, the Shining Ones smiled at the pilgrims.

"Your travels are all but finished. Two difficulties remain to be overcome. Conquer the perilous river and climb the steep hill, and you will be in the Eternal City."

"Go along with us," said Hopeful, "and show us the way."

"We can show you the way," replied the Shining Ones, "but you can travel it only by the strength of your own faith."

They walked on through the fertile garden until they came to a place directly opposite the gate of the Heavenly City. Between the gate and the spot where the pilgrims stood ran a swift river, foaming and swirling between steep banks.

"What!" cried Christian in amazement. "Is there no bridge?"

But they could see clearly that there was none.

"And is there no other way to reach the gate?"

"Yes," answered the Shining Ones. "But only two men have ever taken that other way. Their names were Enoch and Elijah. They lived long ago, and since their day all who have entered the city have done so by swimming. What is more, from now until the end of time, none will reach the Heavenly gate except through the perilous river."

The pilgrims looked again at the rushing water and their minds were filled with doubt and despair.

"Is it the same depth everywhere," asked Christian, "or are some places shallow enough to be forded?"

"The depth varies," replied the golden-robed strangers. "But it does not depend on the place. You will find this river shallow if your faith is strong. But if your belief in the Lord of the City is weak, you will find no foothold to help you, and the current will sweep you away."

There was no choice for the pilgrims. Summoning up

all their faith and courage, they plunged into the river. Its chill waters took their breath away and made their flesh shrink.

"Hopeful!" cried Christian. "My brother! The waves are breaking over my head. I am sinking in deep waters!"

"Be of good cheer, brother," shouted Hopeful above the rushing of the stream. "I feel the bottom, and it gives a firm foothold."

But Christian was not to be comforted.

"Ah, my friend," he cried, "the sorrow of death surrounds me. I shall never see the land which flows with milk and honey, the blessed land of Zion."

Thoughts of his own sinfulness weighed him down. Darkness filled his eyes. He was full of terror in case he should die in the river and never step through the gate into the Celestial City. Visions of hobgoblins and evil spirits haunted him, dancing wildly in his imagination.

Hopeful strove valiantly to keep his companion's head above the foam. Whenever Christian sank down, he bore him up. He spoke encouraging words to him, telling him that a party of angels stood at the gate, waiting to welcome them to salvation.

"Do not lose hope, my dear brother! It is good that you are filled with the thought of your own wickedness. Sinners die laughing, but those who are loved by the Lord think always of their souls' peril. But for us all will be well. We are going to be saved. Only think of that, and keep your spirits up."

Still Christian struggled with the waves, sinking and rising, never going down for long but never striking out bravely for the far shore.

"Think of Jesus!" cried Hopeful. "He will save you, if you call to him!"

Suddenly Christian gave a shout of joy and triumph.

"I see him, I see him! He says: *When you pass through the rivers, I will be with you. When you cross the waters, they will not overflow you.* I know now that I shall reach the shore!"

At this they both took courage. The Devil could do no more. They climbed out on the bank before the gate, safe for ever from his evil-doing.

They were astonished to see that the two Shining Ones awaited them. But in this land of miracles they knew that nothing was too strange to believe. As they stood on dry land once more, the Shining Ones saluted them, saying,

"We are spirits sent to tend those who will inherit salvation. Come with us to the gate and enter."

Christian and Hopeful gazed wonderingly before them. A steep hill rose into the sky, and at its top, so close that they felt they could have touched the diamond battlements of its walls, stood the Celestial City in all its unearthly splendour.

21

The Pilgrim's Conquest

As Christian and Hopeful climbed joyfully towards the Heavenly City, the path became steeper and steeper, until the slope seemed as sheer as the face of a cliff.

"This must be the second difficulty mentioned by the Shining Ones," whispered Hopeful.

"Yes. But my feet find an easy way, and the climb is nothing to me. These two bright angels are helping us. What's more, we left our heavy mortal clothes in the river. Without them, I feeel as light as air."

Although the City was built above the highest cloud, the two pilgrims made their way up through the upper air with perfect ease, talking happily as they went and rejoicing that their journey was almost over. Their glorious companions tried to explain the beauty of the Kingdom they were about to enter, calling it the Heavenly Jerusalem, Mount Zion, and the home of the spirits of just men made perfect.

"But words can never hope to tell of the wonders of the Celestial City," sighed one of the Shining Ones. "When you dwell there, you will see for yourselves. You will wear robes of white and gold; you will eat the never-fading fruit of the Tree of Life; every day you will walk and talk with the Lord himself. All the sorrows you have known in this life will be forgotten. Sickness, suffering and death will be no more."

Christian and Hopeful asked what they would have to do when they arrived in the blessed kingdom.

"No tasks await you, my brothers. The time has come for you to reap the rich harvest you have sown in your days on earth. For the pain you have felt, you will be rewarded with eternal bliss. Joy will take the place of all your sorrows. Crowns of gold will encircle your brows, and you will gaze for ever on the unimaginable beauty of the Lord. In the world you strove to serve him, although a thousand obstacles hindered you. Now your service will be free and glad. You will see him face to face, and his majestic voice will echo in your ears."

"Shall we meet the friends we knew on earth?" asked Christian.

"Those who have arrived before you will embrace you with tears of joy. You yourselves will give a loving welcome to those who follow," replied the Shining One. "As for your enemies, all who opposed you in the world—Hate-good, Flatterer and all that wretched crew—are to be judged by the Lord. When he sits in judgement on them, you will share in his power, and whatever wrong they have done you will be weighed in the scale against them."

The pilgrims and their guides were drawing near the gate. With wondering eyes, Christian and Hopeful saw a company of bright angels coming towards them. Their robes shone and sparkled like the sun on the white foam of a waterfall.

"These two men loved our Lord while they were in the world," said the Shining Ones to the company of angels. "For his sake they left everything they owned and set off on a long and weary pilgrimage. He sent us to fetch them and we have brought them to the gates of the City."

The heavenly host gave a great shout of blessing and

welcome. As their pure voices echoed from the massive walls, a new sound filled the air—the stirring, silver-bright note of a thousand trumpets. A band of trumpeters poured forth from the gates, their instruments glittering in the unearthly light. They shouted a welcome to the pilgrims and then, raising their trumpets to their lips once more, blew a long, exultant blast.

Surrounded by angels and filled with the joy of harmonious music, Christian and Hopeful walked on. Now they saw every detail of the wondrous city walls, brilliant with gems. From the top of every tower in Zion, bells pealed out in welcome. Their joy was so great that they thought themselves in Heaven already. Most marvellous of all was the idea that they too would soon be citizens of the Lord's City, to dwell there until the end of time.

"Look!" cried Christian as they passed through the golden gate. "There is an inscription overhead.

BLESSED ARE THEY THAT DO HIS COMMANDMENTS, THAT THEY MAY HAVE RIGHT TO THE TREE OF LIFE, AND MAY ENTER IN THROUGH THE GATES INTO THE CITY."

Abraham, Moses and the other prophets looked down from the walls, smiling on the newcomers.

"These pilgrims have made their way here from Destruction," one of the angels announced. "Give me your scrolls, Christian and Hopeful, and you will be dwellers for ever in the Celestial City."

The pilgrims took their precious scrolls from their bosoms and handed them to the keeper of the gate. The Lord commanded that they should be allowed to enter. Trembling with joy, they set foot in Zion. As they crossed the threshold they were miraculously transfigured, appearing suddenly in raiment of gold and shining white.

Angels gave them silver harps on which to make music in praise of the Lord. Golden crowns were set upon their brows. As the gates swung open, every street in the city shone like the sun as the light of Heaven was reflected from the golden pavements.

Slowly the gates closed behind the triumphant pilgrims. Winged angels surrounded them, and led them into the presence of the Lord.

Not long afterwards, Ignorance arrived at the far shore of the river. He made the crossing in comfort, for Vain-hope ferried him over. But he had to struggle up the steep hill on his own, for no one came out to meet him, and even when he was close to the gates he had to walk alone.

He knocked impatiently, as if expecting to be let in at once.

"Where are you from?" asked the stern gate-keeper. "What do you want?"

"I have prayed in the Lord's churches, and listened to his preachers in my home town of Conceit."

"And where is your scroll?"

Ignorance hung his head and said nothing.

"Come, my friend. Do you mean to tell me that you have no token to show me? Unless you have some sign, I cannot let you in."

Ignorance still said nothing, so the keeper of the gate sent word to the Lord. But he was feasting with Christian and Hopeful and would have nothing to do with Ignorance. Instead, he sent down the two Shining Ones who had accompanied the pilgrims up the hill. They seized hold of him, bound him hand and foot, and bore him away from Zion. They carried him through the air until they reached the gloomy cave in the rocks which the shepherds had pointed out. This was one of the entrances to Hell: the air was full of the cries of the damned. Ignorance was thrust in at this doorway, and the boulder was rolled back over the entrance.

Christian and Hopeful were at the height of joy and bliss, feasting with the Lord. But they saw that they had never been safe until they were inside the gates, for there was a way to Hell from the entrance to Heaven, just as there was from the City of Destruction.